Henry Hanby Hay

Trumpets and Shawms

Henry Hanby Hay

Trumpets and Shawms

ISBN/EAN: 9783337314965

Printed in Europe, USA, Canada, Australia, Japan

Cover: Foto ©Andreas Hilbeck / pixelio.de

More available books at **www.hansebooks.com**

Trumpets and Shawms

By

HENRY HANBY HAY

Author of

Created Gold and Other Poems

Studies in Shakespeare

etc.

Philadelphia

ARNOLD AND COMPANY

1896

To the Isle of Man

I dedicate this Book

Country and Mother are the twins of one emotion

So when I dedicate these verses, with all love

To Manxland

I include the Dear Mother, that truest

and best of all friends

CONTENTS

INTRODUCTION

MY friend Henry Hanby Hay desires that I should introduce his new poems with a few prefatory remarks. After reading his volume, I can see no other reason why I have been selected to stand even for a moment in front of it than that I am a Manxman, and many of the poems relate to Manxland.

Mr. Hay is a Manxman also, born and brought up and educated in the Isle of Man, still visiting us in the intervals of his professorial vacations, well-known throughout the island and always remembered here with affection, esteem and admiration. Love of country is one of the salient qualities of the Manxman, especially if the necessities of livelihood have carried him to distant countries. Many are the letters that reach me from time to time from Manxmen in far-off lands, and pathetic and deeply touching are some of the peeps which I thereby get into that great human force, the love of country; but I doubt if I have ever met the passion of patriotism more powerfully developed than it is in the author of this beautiful volume.

There is always a deep call to a man's heart from the soil that gave him birth, and the love of country has very pathetic and sometimes very humorous manifestations. I remember that when, some years ago, I was traveling in Iceland, I had for my guide an old Icelander who had never left his native land. One day we were riding side by side over the serried face of that volcanic country, across its broad plains of lava, and past its yawning fissures that looked like the empty vaults of a vast graveyard of the old time that had been left behind and forgotten. And telling myself that surely God had never intended that the foot of man should tread on that desolate land, I turned to the old guide and said, " Jan, have you any children ?" The old man answered " No." " Have you a wife ?" " No." " No relations ?" " No." " Then would not you like to go away to America and make your home with your fellow-countrymen who are settling at Winnipeg ?" There was silence for a moment. Jan looked round on the landscape and then said slowly, " No, sir, I couldn't leave the old country ; it is the fairest land the sun shines upon."

Mr. Hay has better reasons than my old Icelandic guide for thinking his native island the fairest of fair places, but his patriotic love of it is, I do not doubt, quite independent of its beauty—a passion almost as deep as the filial love which he combines with it in his touching dedication.

The Isle of Man as a scene for literary treatment enjoys certain peculiar advantages. The most ardent lover of the little island will not pretend for a moment that its natural scenery is grand or wonderful, but it has a beauty and a charm which some of us, who know the great places of the earth, would not exchange for rarer qualities. Above and beyond this, however, as a subject for poem or story, the Isle of Man has a strange historical interest, and also the dramatic advantage of a material and matter-of-fact present time, upon which the romantic past impinges in a very extraordinary and striking way. We have our old Norse government, founded more than a thousand years ago, still in the freshness of its active life, and on the modern substitute for old midsummer's day our legislators in church and state still hold that open-air parliament which was, perhaps, the earliest recognition of the rights of the people to some form of representative government. Side by side with this romantic past and present so strangely compounded, we have the everyday interests which come of what is called the "visiting industry." Our little island is the holiday resort of a large section of the English people. Something like three hundred thousand tourists and "trippers" from neighboring counties in the "adjacent islands" come to the Isle of Man in the months of July and August for health and recreation. This has had the effect of obliterating much of the primative character of our people, though it has not yet disturbed their old-time institutions. Our home industries have declined, partly perhaps from neglect or the lack of active encouragement, but mainly no doubt, from natural causes over which our people have had little control. The great schools of herrings appear to have deserted our coasts, the invention of the steamship has limited the markets once frequented by our sailing luggers, and the spinning jenny has almost wiped out our manufacture of homespun cloth. Thus the occupations of the Manxmen have changed within half a century from those of a small home-staying race, half fishermen and half crofters, to the very different occupations of active and enterprising lodging-house and hotel proprietors, with their hackney-carriage and pleasure-garden industries, and all the usual and inevitable auxiliaries.

The reader does not desire that I, on my part, should make any literary confidences, but I may perhaps be forgiven if I say that when I myself as a novelist came to consider the Isle of Man as a subject for literary treatment, I saw that it was capable of being dealt with in two very different ways. First, it was possible to treat this romantic little island from the point of view of its legislative and historic interest, with all the daring entanglements of incident and emotion which were embraced thereby—thus floating over it as if it were, so to speak, an island of Prospero. Next, the Isle of Man was capable of being dealt with realistically as a very curious compound of contradictions, of romance and perhaps rather ordinary materialism, of a strange and poetic past and a narrow and unpoetic present.

And if I had been a poet instead of a novelist I think I should have seen that in the same way the island from the poet's point of view is capable of two different lines of treatment. There is the dramatic method to which the Isle of Man beyond most places very properly and powerfully lends itself. To get inside of the life of a little insular community—cut off from the mainland by thirty miles of sea on every side, having its own government, its own church, its own families, society, aristocracy, and poor—is obviously a channel to striking passages of the human story. This method has been adopted by our friend, the Rev. T. E. Brown, who, in " Fo'cas'le Yarns" and other books, has gone to the very heart of the home life of our people, rendering their whims and idiosyncrasies, their dialects and their customs with a fidelity, a pathos and a humour that are entirely beyond praise of mine. Again there is the scenic manner of treating the island in a poem—regarding it, not from within as Mr. Brown has done, but entirely from without. To describe its fairy glens, its amber rivers, its undulating coast, its blue waters, its green hill-tops, its gorse and its cushag and its fuschia, with the human interest as secondary though always present—this also is a hopeful way of approaching the subject.

Of these two methods there can be hardly any question that the dramatic is perhaps, on the whole, and in the long run, the more vital in its interest, but the other method is even more popular, more easily within the sympathy of the outside world; and this is the method which my friend, Mr. Hay, has aimed at in the Manx poems contained in the present volume. All that remains to me to say on that head is that in his descriptive passages relating to the Isle of Man he has given us the very color and scent of our lovely and beloved little island, and that no photograph and hardly any picture, unless it were from the hand of a master, could bring a stronger sense to the stranger, of the scenic qualities which we as Manx people so greatly prize.

For these excellencies of presentation Mr. Hay is sure of the gratitude of all Manxmen who are true lovers of their country, but whether the great English nation that is American will care to con-cern itself any further with the affairs of the little English nation that is Manx, is more than I can dare to predict. I do humbly and sincerely confess to an uneasy feeling that we who are writing about the Isle of Man must seem to be putting it a little out of proportion to the general interests of the universe. If the public shares that feeling occasionally I for my part shall have no right to complain ; but for Mr. Hay I may fairly claim a patient hearing, as for a new speaker who has not tired the ear by previous appeals.

I am fully conscious that I have touched only the fringe of the claims that might properly be made for Mr. Hay's volume, but my function at the moment is by no means that of a critic. If it were so I think it would be easy to show that the poet in this instance has drunk deeply and to much pur-pose from the fount of his master, Robert Browning. It may be that his critics will tell him that in achiev-ing some of the noble qualities of his great original he has annexed a few of the master's defects. I am partly conscious that in some of the poems of this volume a great emphasis and condensation have been secured at a certain cost of lucidity and purity of vehicle. But it is obviously so essential to the poetic medium that the form should be quintessential that the severest critic of language will condone some angularities of style for the sake of compression and power, and that both these great factors are at strong play in many of the pages of this book no one who opens it will, I think, be disposed to question.

English poetry, and I have no doubt American poetry also, has so long carried on what Carlyle called "the troubadour business," that it is a relief from time to time when poets arise who are daring enough to use poetry as a vehicle for the criticism of life. The criticism of life in poetry has great and palpable dangers, and certain of these have been only too conspicuous in the writings of a great American poet whose name does not need to be mentioned in this connection. But where the issues of contemporaneous life have been greatly dealt with in poetry, the results have been great indeed. It would seem to me that the world is growing a little weary of the dreamily romantic which has so long played its part in poetry, and that the realism which has forced itself on the sister art of fiction is beginning to make itself strongly felt in the poetic art as well. This touches a much larger question than I can dare to discuss in so short a space, but perhaps my ultimate feeling would be that in the poem as in the novel, the highest results are to be obtained by the greatest realism of execution, combined with the strongest idealism of conception. That is, as far as I am able to judge, the view taken by my friend Mr. Hay also, as several of the poems in this volume would appear to show. At all events we have in Mr. Hay a poet of very deep and passionate earnestness, fully conscious of the high vocation to which the poet is called, and with ardent aspirations to achievement. That much has been achieved already will be, I think, abundantly clear to the reader of this book, and that still more may perhaps be looked for from one whose knowledge of life is so wide, whose outlook on the world is so broad, whose sympathies are so generous, whose spirit is so true and tender, may I think, be confidently predicted.

Hall Caine.

GREEBA CASTLE, ISLE OF MAN
December 1, 1896

Trumpets and Shawms

TRUMPETS

T HE pealing trumpet shakes the trembling wold !
In rhymer's coil I catch the blare
Of poppied earth and painted air,
The red, red rose, whose redolency grew
When sun's gold fleeces mingled with the dew.
I catch incarnate will when squadrons come,
When scarlet swings to tucket of the drum.
The swimmer's supple limbs against the tide,
The onward when with dancing blood we ride,
The fire car galloping with whirling wheel,
While clangs the tocsin and the axemen reel ;
All these are trumpets, busy, potent, bold,
Whose pealing flourish shakes the trembling wold.

The cricketer, who strikes with muscle strong,
The shrilling black cap, drunk with lusty song,
The scarlet forge where flame's surprises rise and fall,
The great red sun translifting vision to its joyful ball,
The rustic clinging pair who cross the ancient stile,
While bell trips bell and children shrill and smile,
And throw syringa, then the chimes grow bold—
The pealing flourish shakes the trembling wold.

The snow-rush in the Alps when echoes rave,
Rocks shake, beasts tremble, only man is brave.
The cataract—as if God stopped the sea,
Then let it flow—roaring eternally;
The steamship on her calm imperial way,
Mounting great peaks of rugged foaming gray;
Macbeth's gigantic stride, a force unspent,
Announced by mines in music eloquent;
The shouts for volunteers when tempests roll;
These, too, are trumpets, trumpeting the soul.
Till the trumpet of the Lord shall quicken death,
And all that was, unfold
And fill the innumerable spaces of the stars,
Blare, trumpet, blare, and shake the reeling wold.

SHAWMS

The cool soft tinkle of the rill,
The gentle bells when eve is still;
To stand athwart the dust of meal,
While drip, drip goes the mossèd wheel;
The silver sacring at the mass,
Light strained through mignonetted glass;
The hour we dream on joys long past;
Blue morn above the broken mast,
Where gulls preen feathers vexed by storm,
Pipe, blandly pipe, O dulcet shawm!

To swim in silent tepid June
Beneath the weird eye of the moon ;
To briskly tread the crispèd snow
While air is like a tensioned bow ;
A singing boy's keen treble note,
Love trembling in the lover's throat ;
An ancient actor's fitful flame,
The sampler of some feeble dame ;
A little child's seraphic form,
Pipe, blandly pipe, O dulcet shawm !

ANGELO AND THE CARDINAL

THE ancient sculptor sat and mused, his audi-
ence hour had come,
    The sternly purposed face astir with spirit
never dumb.
A morning work, immortal strokes, already earned that
rest ;
The chisel of his age excelled the skill of art's young
best.
From marble he had showered sparks quicker than eye
can shrink,
Frowning at times ; such are the throes when greater
artists think,
And when a hundred things are born, which one life
cannot end.
With ducats from a copper vase he'd helped a needy
friend,
For thus in Godly ways he walked, with Godlike force
to plan ;
All Italy adored his name, revered the good old man.

The bits of marble round the room showed mind at ebb
and flow,
A group of had-been figures carved, then shattered with
a blow,

A blocked-out statue of a saint, three children (incom-
plete),
The Fates, vast giants terrible, bowed women at their feet.
On two glued sheets stood Peter's fane as he desired it
should,
A sketch of Mary childing hearts by her rapt mother-
hood,
A head of Helen, drawn when youth was marching in
Love's train,
A palace front, a giant shape named in the master's brain,
Sketches whose ripeness only asked the nursing care of
years.
Scholars and noblemen stood there with most attentive
ears;
And a cardinal, the drag-net of our holy lord's police;
But Michael dominated all, yet longed for death's release.

He talked—how horizontal lines show out the calm
serene,
How curves express sublimity, what light and shadow
mean,
How awe is shown by simple lines from prettiness
debarred,
How 'neath bright color's flattery the human form is
marred,
How, blanched by thought, the lines relax, the meanest
face refines,
How purity keeps women young by never cording lines.

It seemed creation, this effect at once on ear and sight,
For, 'cross the paper as he spoke, the black chalk swept
    with might.

"In painting men," said Angelo, "the semblance is
    the shard ;
"Wouldst paint the mind?   Mark gait and pose, and
    countenance off guard ;
"These print upon the brain, and when the subject's
    self you see
"Paint, and your canvas soon will throb with motion
    full and free.
"When you can paint soul in the face, be certain, on
    the whole,
"That if you look in any face, that face shall tell its
    soul ;
"Then dip your brush in color vast, and dare the
    prattler's scorn ;
"In transit 'twixt the eye and mind your painting must
    be born.
"Keep sight and fancy ever pure, nor let the soul grow
    numb,
"Then, when you summon incidents, those incidents
    will come.
"Suppose this feeble hand must draw, from memory,
    our Count
"As yesterday, at noon, he stood beside his garden
    fount.

" Behold " (the garden grew as quick as landscape
      which we think)
" Here, on the right," (he sketched), " a girl is lean-
      ing o'er the brink.
" So ! very gentle, flowing curves, her passive faith
      express,
" Eyes not too round, the lower lid an arch of tender-
      ness ;
" Now blend and make the tresses soft, part lips with
      half a sigh ;
" Hands, don't forget they're shaped by mind, re-
      laxed, for love is nigh.

" The Count, disturbed, half turns his head—a strong
      firm outline now,
" A straight line melting to a curve shall shadow forth
      his brow ;
" The nose a straight line, thickening, with bridge not
      pinched, but thin,
" It is a sign of birth, when joined to nostrils curv-
      ing in.
" The lips must close without restraint, a line or two of
      age ;
" See, in the angles of the face, the angle of the
      sage ;
" The eyebrows, just a little arched, close o'er the deep
      set eyes."
The noblemen all started back to see the Count arise.

" The woman who holds sight, not soul,'' said Angelo,
    with spleen,

" Is classic ''—, here he dashed off lines—, all knew
    Rome's doubtful Queen.

" Now to the left," he cried, "drawn close in corner
    far apart,''

(The old man in his burning zeal thought only of his art)

" Sit, surely, four conspirators :'' the Cardinal rose now,

For fear is touching every mouth, suspicion every brow.

" Beasts ! ever since the ancient days, when wolves gave
    such to Rome,

" Within our borders have been bears, and foxes (close
    at home).

" This face an ape's together squeezed, this vulture
    needs but wings ;

" Flat nose, sharp-angled eyes, gashed mouth, this man
    would poniard kings.

" There—'' (dashing strokes).   From entrance the
    Cardinal swept down,

When suddenly a happy spike attached his scarlet gown,

The painter turned, a dozen strokes to right and left he
    made ;

Then, " I'm fatigued," said Angelo, " my fingers have
    obeyed.''

The Cardinal now reached the place, girl, woman,
    Count were there,

And in the corner, draped baboons were talking with
    a bear.

ONE BY THE SEA—A BOY

Scene—Douglas, Isle of Man

John Clare, *who is lecturing on Manx poets, meets* John Kermode *on the sands, and hears the story of his life.*

WHITE sands and glistening ropes of rack left bare
By the sea, lapping around the Refuge Tower,
That tower, which goodness built and Words-
worth praised.
The sun was low, I cushioned on the beach
And let my book on rifted singers wait.
Then, as I rose to go, an old man came,
A wrinkled, careless, peevish, worn old man.
I knew him not, and yet I knew his face ;
For he had sat and frowned the night before,
When I had lectured to a hearty group—
Folks 'tent to hear about their island bards.
His frown aroused me.   Bah !   I'd come to dream,
And so I turned again to my Manx book
Of golden wreckage, drenched with salt despair,
And read again.   A shadow dimmed the page—
" Alpha, the Angel."   Then a thin voice piped,
" I am John Kermode, and that book is mine.

" Last night you called me ' Poet.'   Well, it needs
" No ghost of meagre, copyrighted books,
" Spider-wise twisted from the author's soul,
" And bound by loveless nights and pinching days,
" To certify a poet.   Pearls there be,
" Sea-bosomed, shelled, whose rosy, nacreous cells
" Are opaline as early winter's sky.
" Good pearls ; but best, as earth goes, set in crowns.
" So, heartily, I thank you for your praise,
" Both praise and blame.   You read my verse last
      night :
" By complaisance you joined my song to theirs.
" My verse is some rose-gall, a curious freak,
" Fit for the fingers of some servant faun.
" Or, as you taste the oyster's pulp and cry,
" ' A pearl, by Jove ! not bad, and mine the find,'
" So the maimed gem has setting at your hands.

" You praised my poem, said the core was sad,
" The bitter ashes of a life misspent.
" Well, I suppose you'll speak of it again,
" Praise it ? so take its story for your fee.
" I want to tell you all that shaped and made
" The thousand grapes, pressed by the hand, Mistake,
" Into the bitter chalice I have drunk.
" What does the poem mean ?   It means my life.

" I close my eyes and face the setting sun,
" And with my shadow, so my thoughts slip back.

" I see a bow-bent bay, an old red pier

" Set in a cold and ever restless sea.

" Behind the pier, the cluttered market-place,

" Hemming a stunted church ; and round the church

" A dozen cart-wide, elbow-bending lanes,

" With corners safed by old guns set on end.

" Some yards beyond, there comes the wall-flower's scent,

" Contending with the smell of herring cured,

" Oak chips and salted fish, and burning pitch.

" Oft have I edged across the market-place :

" Conger and turbot, lobster too, and crab,

" And gaping codfish flung upon the stones ;

" Behind the skate and flounder, flowers, rough-
    bunched ;

" Poppy, sweet-william, canterbury-bell,

" Dog-rose, St. John's-wort, scarlet pimpernel ;

" And thus it was the blue-eyed people talked :

" ' The wind is north, the steamer will be late,'

" ' Good rain and hot, the strawberries need drink,'

" ' Herrings at three a penny ! ' so it went.

" Oh God ! was this shrunk hand once smooth with
    youth,

" With eager youth. What joyful ignorance

" Was mine, composed of awe and wonderment.

" The brawling boatman, hand upon his knife,

" I shrunk from him, to listen, with large eyes,

" To Cheap Jack's lies, to me, unfathomed facts.

" Jar shocked me, as the ermine shrinks from
      dirt—
" Not yet had life's intruders broken in.
" The first, fate sent.   O, cursèd pride of rank !
" A man-made gulf, where nature meant a line.
" To be a man in England, that is good !
" But 'tis—to be an English gentleman—
" An absolute of dominant repose.
" The sedentary shopman envies most
" The rich man's privilege of being clean,
" His pleasant ordered person, his fresh air,
" The drowsy sweetness of his nurturing.

" To be a laborer is bearable :
" He has his duties and his appetites,
" But to approach, catch at, and never reach,
" To hunger in the presence of the feast,
" To have the slumberless ' not proven ' writ,
" The Scottish verdict whispered 'gainst your life,
" ' O, good enough, not quite a gentleman !'
" Is to be quicksand caught, while love stands near ;
" ' Not quite ' the shears which clip content away,
" And send men shivering across the fields.

" My life should have a worse intruder yet,
" One borne across life's threshold by myself :
" The shallow wisdom of a bubble world.
" Unhappy ?   No ! At sixteen life was sweet.

" My father kept the inn, and, of the two,

" He labored most; his son was not his drudge,

" But something to be coshered by his toil.

" An old lieutenant, housed by him for years,

" Had left him books; and all these books were
  mine !

" With greedy joy I read them, good and bad,

" Then to our attic, barn, and garden-plat,

" I swift transplanted all the bookish folk :

" Crime in the attic, revellers in the barn,

" But queens and damsels nigh the fuchsia-bed.

" Sometimes I anguished to the brink of tears,

" And sometimes choked to free myself with words.

" And then I let the lightning hurry down

" The broken lilt of some remembered song.

" My puzzled father heard, but never blamed.

" Love says, ' He's right !' thus helps to make us
  right.

" The town-folks grinned, because a churl resents

" The power which puzzles him, or sneered, ' half-
  baked !'

" I lived with Quentin Durward, not with them ;

" Had Madge's breast (no, not forgotten, Madge !)—

" A little, tireless bit of utter love :

" Big eyes, a crinkle in the blue-black hair ;

" The penny of the eagle and the child

" We'd broke in twain, and sworn ' to be as true

" ' As the trout's backbone centers in the trout.'

" I found expression, when I tasted love,

" Agates are found, where we untreasure gold.

" My verse, my blossoms, had the sun of praise.

" Upon their leaves no critic insects crawled.

" No beetle nipped my roses for his food.

" The village paper printed all I wrote :

" Poor notes, but mine ; the black-cap sang his own.

" What days ! so large, so innocent, so true !

" Joy best appraises values, after all.

" In warm, sweet June, my little book was born.

" My father's purse had wrought the miracle.

" Friends bought it, and our guests, too, bought and
    praised.

" Madge and her mother dwelt beyond the town,

" Their cottage, almost hidden by the hills ;

" Small, but it filled my soul.   I see it yet—

" A tall geranium filling up the panes,

" The tea-things ready for the homely meal ;

" Upon a chest of drawers the Bible lay ;

" There was the hollow fire-place, with its hook,

" With sweet turf smoking on the ample hearth.

" Back of the house, a little, whitewashed room,

" All sweet with salted rose-leaves, was for me.

" When June came round again, all was for me.

" Before the hazy hearth, we sat and planned.

" We planned our wedding and our wedding feast—

" How, Burns-like, I would make the isle renowned,

" How we would help the old man at the inn,

" And how—Madge nodded—we would have six boys.

" One night I came back, all aglow, from her

" Through lanes, with tall ferns high above my head.

" I reached the inn, and rested on the porch,

" And heard two voices, then I heard my name.

" It was a famous noble and his wife.

" At length she said, ' Hear what the " Record " says.'

" Her voice was mellow, warm with motherhood.

" And (see, 'tis yellow now,) read what she read :

> *This singer has the potency of growth, he has a*
> *voice ; now let him sing his song. Matter is booked,*
> *and always possible, but manner is the free, full gift*
> *of God. So let him don his russet, cut a staff, and*
> *buy experience ; even love the world, if he will only*
> *hate its livery.*

" Then came quotations in a long array,

" Jewels which made a precious thing more rich.

" 'O, Hugh !' she said, ' this is but half the truth !

" ' This yeoman-bard has no imperious need

" ' To check his life or falsify his song.

" ' He is a picture, framed in simpleness ,

" ' For when we owe a debt to luxury,

" ' Soon are we grinding in Philistia's pens.

" ' I see a freeman, when I see him walk,

" ' His sweetheart's head just level with his heart.

" ' A sea-pink, pressed against a boulder's breast !'

" ' A pity, aye, a pity,' answered Hugh,
" ' That he should lack the polish of the world,
" ' The gentle stimulus of women peers !
" ' How he might make men tremble with his pen !'
" ' Dear Hugh,' she said, ' when satirists are made,
" ' A poet, think ! a poet is undone !'
" ' Won't poverty,' he answered, ' carbonize
" ' His diamonds to boil next Tuesday's broth ?'

" I felt the eagle-poison flush my brain.
" In that proud hour I hungered for the world.
" To know the world, what is it, but to know
" A million sneers, a thousand verging crimes ?
" To make a platform of our meanest self,
" From thence to preach the creed of levelling.
" Which crops the good, and stake-supports the ill ?
" A traitor net should drag me to that world.
" What made that net ?   The triple thread : myself,
" The poison in my heart, and summer dead.
" For winter blurs our isle out of the world.

" The inn was guestless, half its doors were barred,
" And shuttered windows spake of gloom within.
" The stables, too, were bare ; the attic, cold,
" And stupor gyved the freedom work allowed.
" Grim months, lorn weeks, made up of dreary
        days.
" With what sick hate, I went forth every morn !

" What weary, wan, and tired morns they were,
" 'Neath the cold shadows of the narrow streets !
" I went o'er roads of rain-soaked, cloggy clay,
" With now and then a draggled hurry-by.
" And yet the rain was best.   It beat my face.
" A storm had been a joy, but oh ! that mist,
" That white, remorseless, cruel, clinging mist !
" The cruel gray of unimpassioned hate !
" When mist went back and sunbeams filtered through,
" I walked the wet, brown sands, and sought for peace.

" Before me foamed the dirty, leaden sea.
" I splashed through wavelets, all the beach was lone,
" Slipped on the weeds, broke with my stick the ice,
" Which thinly filmed the pools among the rocks :
" For it was cold, but not so very cold.
" High seas, and hurricanes, and bitter cold
" Were better than the mist, and drip, and chill.
" Thrice every week I hurried to the pier,—
" The old red sandstone, wash'd clean by the rain,—
" And waited with a dumb expectancy.
" Till far off came a grumble, then a sob,
" Then, red and blue, the lights burned through the fog,
" And the slow steamer drifted to my sight.
" A shout, a hawser thrown, a little crowd,
" And then with dragging feet I sought the inn.
" Why not that cottage, 'neath the rough-browed hill
" Far from the sob-lashed leaping of the sea,

" Out of the wind, nay, if sea voices came,
" Their rude roar fell to cozy lullabies,—
" There nested, with two angels, warmth and love,
" My wavy-haired, my all-life, little Madge,
" The sweetest woman woman ever bore !
" Why not ?   The rough, fierce liquor of the world
" Had killed the taste for noble fruit and bread.
" I feared her eyes ; not yet that baser state,
" When I should hate the innocence I wronged.

" One day she wrote ; coarse strokes, and yet, if truth
" Gave outward signs, each stroke was beauty's curve.
" O, yes, I went ; hoping, ' Perhaps she means
" ' To quarrel.'   Men's careers are more than love.
" Just as I reached the door, she raised the latch.
" How trifles mark the climax of each pain.
" I know she wore a something touched with red.
" And look ! the old gun swings against the beam,
" Herring, the score, are stacked and hung to dry,
" And o'er the scarlet of the living fire,
" A mighty caldron glugs and purrs content.

" I filled her hearth, I tasted of her cup,
" I gave her, too, a proper Judas kiss ;
" And then—there are such poverties of shame,
" They will be stammered at the Judgment Day—
" I sneered at her rough hands, her faded shawl,
" The herring smell, the fashion of her hair.

" In wounding her, I bestialized myself.

" Ere insults had been reached, I anguished, too.

" When winging lark, with broken pinions falls,

" Not all at once the empyrean joy is lost ;

" But when the earth is reached, 'tis shapeless doom.

" She shut her sense against the pelt of words,

" And answered, ' John, you came to say " good-bye."

" ' Don't quite forget me, and I shan't forget

" ' The afternoon we first kept company.

" ' You kissed me in the meadow, by the oak,

" ' Your father's horses scurried 'cross the field.

" ' God bless you, John !   Best sleep with us to-night,

" ' For mother'll find her tongue, if you go home.

" ' The bed is made, and I'll unlace your shoes.'

" She knelt before me, pulling out the lace.

" My tears burst forth, and dropped upon her hair.

" She did this homely service not for me,

" But for the noble man I might have been ;

" For, home, and nuptial bliss, and babes unborn,

" Alas, alas ! I murdered, but she blessed.

" Not one sharp word.   God blew the mist away,

" That I might see my filthy, naked crime.

" Next morn, before she stirred, I sneaked away ;

" Shall I not see that better part again,

" When the death-damps are cold upon my brow,

" And soul to life's first citadel returns ?

" God grant, that with the olden sights and sounds,

" Her first-time smile may come, but not the tear !

" When love, the fellowship, has voided soul,
" Nor faith, nor hope, abideth in a man.
" And yet I had my rouse of prosperous days.

" Lord Hugh acknowledged me, allowed my claims.
" O, I suppose, I was his Frankenstein !
" Pride lifens what our condescension shapes.
" My verses, too, like sea-weed stretched and dried,
" Still kept their sea-pool tint and smacked of salt.
" The city papers praised the peasant's song.
" I found myself within historic gates.
" My lady's parrot and my lord's Bernard
" Had place there, too, and so had savage spears,
" And burnished blades and barbarous bits from Ind.
" The splendid rooms, soft-tinted, full of light ;
" The giant vases, and the pale, sweet bloom,
" The shiny wood, carved gems, and oldtime gold,
" The vast array of flashing forks and spoons,—
" All these, at least, I could confront unawed.
" In the old inn, I'd ordered waiters, too,
" Footmen, past masters of these mysteries.

" At first, the women made me move askance ;
" I could not fancy them with common needs,
" Filled with our bitter-sweet humanity :
" White hands, and waxy order ; trailing robes
" Of frost-blown lace ; a nameless drowsy scent ;

" And restful voices, freighted with right words ;

" Their soft hair showing 'gainst my bristling beard ;

" Their soft silks neighboring my shining black ;

" Their slim hands shaming mine, mine, good to toil ;

" Or, once it happed, to tug the life-boat oar.

" My shame-flush passed, for soon the women smiled,

" Because in women, worship cannot die ;

" Turned from the stars, it wastes itself in pugs.

" But while my lyrics pleasured womanhood,

" They could not spice the public hours of men.

" My hard-got gifts were what they most contemned,

" My blush confronted centuries of ease,

" I flamed with thought, while coolness was their creed,

" Their bagatelles disowned my earnestness.

" Each mortal has some final, last resource,

" Something which nature keeps for desperate needs ;

" Too oft it is the evil of his good.

" To make this final thing a use, is mad !

" It is to toss your precious things, brocades,

" And gems, and pictures, books, and massy plate

" To the fierce rioters, who, whetted thus,

" Press on the more, and shatter house and life.

" I could not move them.   I would make them laugh !

" I broke my dainty fancies at their feet.

" Treasures of former days of hope and faith

" Were sport for smoking-room obscenities.

" One night I went.—The brandy spur had passed ;
" And nothing but a dogged dullness stayed.
" Already on my senses beat the smell
" Of the foul slum which hovelled me by day ;
" When H— (the baronet) came striding past,
" And halted me just underneath the lamp.
" ' I've read your book, sir poet,' so he said,
" ' The noble things you could not help but write.
" ' You've put a score of carvings on fame's shelf,
" ' And every night for us, you jig one down.
" ' You cannot catch our light, insidious ease ;
" ' Our fore-bears paid for it, and we still pay,
" ' In books unread, or " the best sayings " skimmed,
" ' In the first sweetness of the morning, lost
" ' In choking heat, and utter emptiness.
" ' I, in my better hours (which happen, too),
" ' Have loved your book, and might have loved the
         man,—
" ' The peasant, who, brain-patent writes down duke.
" ' Pardon ! none take their wisdom from a clown.

" ' One word—I sail to-morrow,—shall be killed,
" ' Or shall ascend the mountains of the moon.
" ' Don't laugh, but sneer, if you must live with us ;
" ' You cannot tickle us, but you can sting.
" ' A cynic is a poet turned to gall.
" ' Men fear the lynx, who only tease the cat.
" ' Rap all, and cudgel some one every night.

" ' Hate-fear contains one element—respect!
" ' The man bruised yesterday, joins you to-day,
" ' Expectant of his neighbor soundly drubbed.
" ' If you must be boy-bishop for the nonce,
" ' Must rule an hour (yourself, and not your book),
" ' Then take my civil, devilish advice.'

" O, good advice! plain, devilish advice!
" To bid the captain at his moorings cut
" His cable into skipping-ropes and knouts.
" Behold! the spirit-power to see men's souls
" With a fiend-power is twined to mock at them.
" Mocking became the business of my life.
" I conquered. From the first I brought to jeer
" The absolute devotion poets use.
" I made this potent master, satire's slave,
" Besides, I chose my ground, I drew them on
" From the great world to greater world of books.

" At length, O, hapless hour! I loved. I loved
" With my brain's heart. I'd loved Madge with
    heart's brain.
" My love had, doubtless, first of hope and fear,
" Long hours of pain, briefs of deliciousness.
" I think it had this universal train;
" For all love has. Mine—take some woman-toy
" Of fragrant leather, silk-lapped, mechlin-edged,
" And throw it on the fire: in puff of flame

" Go silk and lace, and in your grasp remains
" A nauseous, useless, curved, and shameful thing.
" My shame! Let not this trope point blame at her.
" To blame would be my sinker down to hell;
" Yet her sweet graciousness was mine, was mine.
" The lily is not compromised, because
" She benisons the beggar at the gate.
" Nay, not a beggar.   I was something more.
" I brought some element which lilies use.
" I searched her eyes, rejoiced because I found
" Much pity and a little wistfulness.

" I read the text aright, its meaning, wrong.
" Her pity was not for herself, but me.
" She longed as Madge, when Madge unlaced my shoe.
" At length I spake, poured love with fervid voice,
" While fancy, guide-like, ran ahead of speech,
" Turning to fair conclusions, hasty words.
" I told her much; no doubt I kept back part.
" I told her of my birth, small means, and Madge.
" She answered me at once (in voice and mien),
" Her sweet and even gentleness meant, ' nay '
" Long before courtesy allowed the word.
" Then I began to plead—a blockhead plan!
" Honey is gall, when dropped by those unloved,
" While love's blunt sayings are Chrysostom's way;
" And ' why?' I urged, with fluent folly, ' why ' ?
" She paused a little, and her face grew pale,

" And then she put her little hand in mine,

" The soft, firm hand, the little, tingling hand,—

" ' Because I'll wound you, let my hand touch yours.

" ' I think with pleasure of your early days,

"'' There's nothing mean in the rough leaves which guard

" ' The plant-head, till it bloom in fitting time,

" ' And you are—never since Saul drove the plow,

" ' Do I believe, there walked a comelier man.

" ' I'd seen, before I saw the island-prince,

" ' His precious casket, full of island-pearls,

" ' Rare shells and coral, strangely-scented woods.

" ' And when I saw you—nay, I will be brave,—

" ' The floods of life swelled up above their banks,

" ' And for a moment almost channelled forth,

" ' To water pleasant lands called by your name.

" ' O, do not speak ! the water has returned,

" ' To keep one course forever to the sea.

" ' Your arid life choked back my swelling stream.

" ' I might have loved the peasant, so I think ;

" ' I could not love the scoffer.   Friend, return.

" ' Go to your isle, where all God's first intentions
      bloom,

" ' Look nature in the eyes, be simple, true, and live.

" ' Yours is the ferment of the noble wine.

" ' Some poet said that faith is hope grown wise.

" ' And charity is truth, but truth in flower.

" ' Let me believe that my young love which died,

" ' Indeed, saw nobleness delayed, not lost.'

" She lives unwed ; but nobleness was lost.

" Whether my gift was but a local tint,

" A child that died, torn from its island breast,

" I know not ; but that early fancy lost

" Had no successors with imperial crowns.

" Lord Hugh is dead; I live his pensioner.

" Daily I sit and gaze, upon the waves,

" And dream myself, ' One by the sea, a boy.' "

ALPHA, THE ANGEL WHO MAKES

THE inner life obeyed first gave life's bent :
　　　Down in the fissures of the earth I went,
　　　And gathered pebbles in the early morn,
Hard-angled stones, but glints in them were born ;
'Neath white crustacean slumbered rainbow tints,
Which had a joy surpassing moon-charged flints.
Then from the upland's edge smooth voices cried,
" Climb up, no longer in the gloom abide !"
" Hither, strong sovereign," softer voices chimed,
" The shining shadows race to-day "——I climbed,
Upward I climbed the common, well-worn track,
The heavy wallet jolting at my back.
I saw the upland with a sudden thrill,
And half my burden scurried down the hill.
And now there dawned upon my wondering sight
Globules and legion points of colored light.
Mine was the bliss we sometimes have in dream ;
I had a fresh delight in each new gleam.
Again I climbed, the level earth I knew,
Delight had fled, the sun had dried the dew.

Some grief was mine, but e'er emotion died,
" See ! see ! the shining shadows race," they cried.
As sudden as the flash which cows the eye,
Now here, now there, the shadows hurry by ;

A voice came near me as I paused, afraid,
"The games begin, be bold, my fellow-shade."
Truth, shaped by beauty, tenanted the plain,
It strained my being to its highest strain,
"Who stones the essence?" rang out voices sweet,
"His guerdon be the clover at his feet,
"Whose taste brings visions where all shapes assume
"Phantoms of beauty fringed by phantom bloom."
I heard the crash of catapulted stones,
And pride became the marrow of my bones.
Against that shape, of all divineness born,
I hurled the latest pebbles of the morn.
Awful its brow.　I hurled the final stone,
Down sank the sun, and I was left alone !

Alpha, the angel, now discerned by me,
Required the treasures of the morn.　Quoth he :
"Where is the adamant ?　What have you done?"
" I saw the dew-drops cease before the sun."
"Youth gathers treasure ; where is now thy gain ?"
" I saw the shadows chase across the plain."
" Thyself a shade."　" The precious jewels shed
" May yet be gathered ?"　So, at length, I said :
" My soul made earnestness."　He cried, " Too late !
" Another gathers them ; for him I wait !"

THE SINGER, HIS CONTENT

SHALL I ask pity, when mine own I scorn?
    For he who sings must sigh. Let it be mine
    To bear the burden of all woes, to mourn
With lightning-smitten elm and blasted kine,
With brook's frustration, robin's ruined home;
For in this dread and ominous debate
I drive the panting furrows through the loam,
Glad to do service for my rich estate.
Shall I revolt, then, 'gainst my diadem
And let the burden, honor, questioned be,
Knowing that grief distilleth many a gem,
The jewels of mine immortality?
Not mine the miracles of Moses' rod;
Yet I interpret too 'twixt man and God.

KING ANANIAS

LOVED yet scourged him, cutting words
 And phrases are my staples :
Less brightly shines the sun ; he's dead,
 This beggar tramp of Naples.
He was a poet ! Keep the word,
 A Poet in his dreaming ;
But dreams not once compressed to thought,
 Nor shaped to form and seeming ;
A pack of things incongruous,
 Of colors blending never ;
For though he did not write a line
 He planned designs forever ;
Trenched on one gift like marble steps
 Of palace not erected,
No wonder that he bade men list
 To him as he elected.
The lyre of old Herodotus
 He played, strange figments teaching.
And one day having conned a text,
 Announced he'd done much preaching.
One grain of solid fact he mixed
 With nineteen grains of fancy.
Ornate in manner with Miss Blanche,
 Ornate to red-cheeked Nancy.

Some laughed at him as he went by.
Some jeered ; none cared to shove him.
I know I always saw his faults,
Until I ceased to love him.
His day ! Rose-trees a future have ;
No future has a fossil.
His nights ! Ne'er chanced, but if they had,
What nights of wit and wassail !
Our little knot in Marti's haunt,
Collected round a table,
He, clad in cambric, superfine,
And English cleric sable,
With Thackeray's and Bulwer's Ghosts,
One right, one left hand, sitting
Attentive to his lightest word,
The viands spiced and fitting,
Then on the wainscot let appear,
In its concise completeness,
His unwrit essay, "Lamb,"—"Montaigne,"
Unique in wit and sweetness,
And his brief poem, crisp and bright,
So full of youth and gladness,
That as he chants it, line by line,
'Tis perfect up to sadness.
With wreath of myrtle dipped in wine,
As prince of "might be" crown him.
Let him repeat one earnest prayer,
Then with rose-water drown him ;

Write on his tomb this epitaph,
   " Here sleeps nor sage nor lover,
" The King of possibilities
   " Lies 'neath this verdant cover.''
Ah, well-a-day, all rainbows fade ;
   Truth lean and uncompassioned
Has puffed away the gilded clouds
   Which " might have been '' had fashioned.
And I must write what really happed ;
   His pleasant art of dyeing
He lost, his hand would fumble with
   His master-key of lying.
My laughing pen is dripping tears,
   For something seems to come, tug
At my heart's strings, the growing old
   Of this poor pompous humbug.
The garb he wore of thought and things
   Was always shining shoddy,
Now hung in rags, and useless rags,
   Rent by the puffed-up body.
His very face deserted him,
   His gloom threadbared his funning,
And fancy's thin mask crumbled up,
   And in its place came cunning.
I wonder whether in those nights
   Complexioned with forever,
When false lights fade, and truth stands bare
   Without the wig called clever ;

I wonder whether faces came,
  A sweetheart or a mother,
Or—Oh, not that—his pinchbeck self
  And spirit faced each other.

SHAKESPEARE ON LONDON BRIDGE

WHEN every one essayed to know,
  And very few essayed to teach,
Ere grammar's rules, like wires stretched
    To trip the feet of nimble speech;
I found myself Will Shakespeare's guest,
  Mine were his ways, his crownèd thought.
I wrapped him like his atmosphere,
  Partook of all he saw and sought.

"A lad of mettle! slow but firm!"
  Stout wrestlers thought, who looked at him.
At rounded neck, and nourished chest,
  And every easy-muscled limb.
Women who gazed, first dreamt, then glowed,
  O'er olive cheeks, carnation spread;
Ripe lips, where purpose watched with love,
  And every maid was rosy red
That felt the brilliant hazel spell
  Of dark, soft eyes, as he passed by,
One hand clutched at the oval chin,
  When, with the breeze, his cap blew high,
Each maiden, and the morning, saw
  The silky toss of chestnut hair,
The lofty wonder of the brow,
  Unruffled, placid, white and fair.

Past windmill, pond, and ancient cross,
　A palace low mid fen and tree,
A gabled house, with dolphins carved,
　With boys disporting nakedly,
A ruined church, fat native weeds
　Grew where the priest had droned Amen,
A heavy coach goes logging by
　And creaks across the hurdles—then
A clamor comes, a river shines,
　Some lead a dripping, muzzled bear;
A bride goes past, with laughing friends,
　A bride expectant, flushed and fair.
Here, raised upon a broken tomb,
　The antic juggles with his knife,
This is the Bankside, this the Thames,
　And this the surging, shouting life,
The busy, bubbling, bustling tide
　Of England, full of fight and cheer,
The breeding, cudgel-playing folk,
　Who whistle, drink, and dine.　Lo here
Is Paris Garden, by my faith
　What mobs are surging through the door!
O'er shout of folks and yelp of dogs,
　The angry bull sends up his roar.
The men are full of sap and meat,
　Are rude and strong, are stout and red;
The comely women, fat and fair,
　Are quick to woo, and swift to wed.

He sees with meditative step
    Black gowns, young curves 'neath jerkins old ;
The gilded sword, the high-peaked hat,
    The ruff and shirt deviced with gold.

    *   *   *   *   *

Across the flood a splendid church,
    A strong-walled town, with many a gate ;
And gardened mansions line the stand
    Where wherries start and barges wait.
We do not come to—we are nigh
    (As in a common nightly dream)
A clumsy street above the flood,
    A bridge of houses o'er the stream.
We cross (spiked heads above us grin),
    An armèd barge darts 'neath our feet ;
The river's gay with boat and swan ;
    Its foaming current shakes the street.
He paused upon the central arch,
    Below raved waters swift and stern,
Yet like his thoughts those waters went
    To circle earth and then return.

Eastward, perforce, our eyes must turn,
    Bombard, deep moat—the grim walls ring
That prison-palace of the world,
    The background stern, of time and king.

We glance at books 'neath swinging signs,
  Love broils of hot Italian days,
The history of English kings,
  Then at the living books we gaze.
How 'cross the bridge these volumes stream,
  Some fast, some slow, some very slow.
The fencing-master sounds his drum,
  A troop of nobles spurring go.
The morice dancer with his mob,
  The spark, with falcon trained to fly,
The beggar at the cart-tail writhes,
  Churls loiter, 'prentices run by.

On last night's stage he talked with peers
  And captains bold from far Cathay,
And now he quips with wholesome grooms
  And people of the work-a-day.
He asks the weaver of his yarn,
  The joiner of his rough-hewn beam,
He notes the casks of Alicant,
  Swung from the pinnace in the stream.

He hears the huckster-woman brawl,
  He speaks the rover rolling nigh,
He gives the reveller, not his heart,
  But keeps him in his ear and eye.
The urchin smiles, for this man knows
  All boyish games and youthful stress,

He knows the child, he knows the lad
    With boyhood's clumsy tenderness.
Unchecked by self, his mind receives,
    And sets in order things terrene ;
All life like Peter's net he holds
    And nothing common nor unclean.
The love-weak girl whose conscience is
    The only witness of her stain,
He knows her as she softly goes
    And judges her in heart, not brain.
So sure his foot, so bright his eye,
    The butcher's dog wags tail to him.
He nothing hates, although he marks
    A hundred faces mean and grim,
And yet within his mind remain
    These faces craft or passion stirred.
When misers throw away their gold,
    Then he'll forget an uttered word.
Each image sinks from sight to soul ;
    For there unchanged he keeps each scene,
Till fitting time, then in the eyes
    They landscape as they first had been,
He sees the truth so perfectly,
    That what he says perforce is true.
His is the blessing of the sun,
    It lights a flower and warms it too.
He saw all things and he saw more,
    He saw the shaping of the stroke,

He saw the mast yet in the green,
And on the bridge his musings woke.

   *   *   *   *   *

Two hours it seemed we stood and gazed ;
Less keen my glance, dissolving slow,
More groups of men and women passed.
He knew them, as a God might know ;
For mien to him meant open soul ;
Where nothing secret might escape ;
Nor swifter sight to find the ore,
Than mind to stamp it into shape.

On London Bridge he caught his souls,
And silked them in the garb, romance.
And made them rest or flutter fierce,
Tangled in nets of circumstance.
What did it seem ?   A narrow way,
An actor scanning London's flow.
All time, with its bemillioned folk,
Has watched since then this magic show.

THE LOWEST OF HEAVEN AROSE

THIS truth shall shine when ten thousand codes
    Are laid on Time's dusty shelf;
The love thou givest thy neighbor shall be
    As the love thou givest thyself.
In it are the shapings of plenty and hope,
    'Tis the womb of things peaceful and true,
'Tis the highest gift of the Christian,
    'Tis the lofty lore of the Jew.
'Twas told near the mighty Nilus,
    By the Pharaoh of long ago;
And the Sheik of the desert lives it,
    When he shares his salt with a foe.
It has little to do with achievements,
    Who has it may never succeed.
It is not denied to doubting,
    But it is denied to greed.
'Tis the knell of all feudal customs,
    'Tis the death of division and clan;
And the outcast may reach it, but never
    The sect-bound and politic man.
'Tis the mighty diffuser of knowledge;
    What I know my other shall share,
And it led me on to a vision,
    Which blew back the veil of the where.

      *   *   *   *   *

There was nothing of sight nor feeling,
　There was nothing of land nor sea,
But a question which must be answered,
　Which wrested the truth from me.
As of old I answered my mother
　Her whisper of, "tell me the whole,"
To the joy of that succor immortal,
　I yielded the strain of my soul.
"I have hoped, and battled, and lusted:
　"The gamut which all men must run.
"O, mighty confirmer and righter of souls,
　"Some things I have never yet done!
"I have glossed with lies no downways of sin,
　"No fool made by God did I pelt.
"I've thrown no dust in the crucible pure,
　"Where the ores of the Genius melt.
"I did not spray men with my own selfish gall,
　"I've fasted from envy and guile,
"I've never fed hope with a starving of praise,
　"I have used all the feasts of a smile."
There fell a swift joy on my hungering soul,
　The loose of a spirit long pent.
As swift as the peal at the heels of the flash
　So swift to the heavens I went.
The gain of one's soul is the gain of all souls,
　The last drop o'erfloweth the cup,
So when I had entered that heavenly midst,
　The lowest of heaven rose up.

As ether is made when the acid comes near,
  What never has been comes to birth,
The lowest of heaven a higher had gained
  By humanity brought from the earth.
Because I had loved all the children of men,
  Usurping no other man's place,
I rose in my longing, my craving for good
  And drew up the heavens a space.
For this I had given up pleasure and gain,
  For this was I careless of fame;
To be in His Presence in more than a light,
  The life and the warmth of a flame.

POTENTIALLY AN ODE

MY BLOOD is hot with this poem—
    I know I shall sing my best ;
'Twill rank with " Moore at Corunna,"
    With " Auld Lang Syne," and the rest
Of poems which come to the hearer
    Like rain to a thirsty crew :
Till men, as the thoughts melt through them
    Acknowledge and love me too.
Majestically strong is my subject,
    Here many a poet fails.
This ship's too leaden, that schooner
    Too weak for her great white sails.
Too often the singer dispenses
    His gold when his love would suffice,
Or drowns the faint balm of the bird-land
    In chants and the burning of spice.
Alas ! for the perfume of metre,
    Alas ! for swift thought and its blaze,
The image has died in its shaping ;
    The figment is lost in its phrase.
On the drear walls of chill language
    Show faintly our fancies, and e'en
In the mirror of even a Petrarch
    His thought's simulacre is seen.

To those who are feeling and loving
This ode has a rapture all clear,
But chanted it shall not be ever
For nations and dullards to hear.

WHEN THIS DRY STAFF WAS GREEN

*[For the sake of my dear niece, Ethel Hay, of Woodville,
near Binda, New South Wales, I dared this poem.]*

THERE'S a staff in the town of Sydney
  Where the flag of the empire spreads
Over the giant harbor,
  Away to the great twin heads ;
Over the beauteous haven
  Where the sails of the earth are furled,
Out to the smoke of the liners
  Away to the under world.
Iron heart of the iron bark
  What have you known in the green?
Staff of the standard which never goes back,
  Speak me the sights you have seen.

The star-built cross at the even,
  Glints of eternal snow,
Years of June and December,
  Seasons of shiver and glow.
Always the snow-fed river
  Flashing adown the vale ;
Smellful trees when the daylight
  Dumbs the crake of the quail—

Dumbs the dirge of the possum,
   Flying, the squirrels have scurred :
In the kiss of the sun, earth is singing,
   As if every beam found a bird.

Flocks of birds in my branches—
   Parroquets flaming along,
Bits of rainbow in motion,
   Droppings of honey in song.
Hark, 'tis the magpie beginning,
   Pleased with its own bold flight,
Pleased with a mirthful gladness,
   Sounds distilled from delight ;
Chanting till some bird answers,
   Barking to rouse the rest—
Ha ! ha ! ha ! goes another,
   Filled with the magpie's jest,
Till all the bush is ringing,
   Merry with joy elate,
Even the black man, rousing,
   Sharply " cooeys " his mate.

Shots are rousing the forest,
   Shouts and a heavy tread,
Tread of the marching Briton,
   Crawling, the savage has fled.

On ! with the dust clouds blowing,
   Cracking of whips for drums,
Music of bull and heifer,
   Toiling, an empire comes.
Words of the foraging Briton
   Soon shall the leatherhead cry,
Soon in the rest of my shadow
   Stockyard and cottages lie.

     *   *   *   *   *

In anguish rose each timber,
   A thousand years of care
Were crowded in a lifetime.
   What did the English bear?
Drought till the green had vanished,
   And streams had ceased to flow,
Drought from the heat of summer
   To winter's edge of snow,
Drought till the kine were fleshless,
   And every wild thing tame,
When over dumb, faint anguish
   Was drawn the scythe of flame.

Sparks in the powdered grasses
   Crept like an infant's hand
Till arose—and the day had vanished—
   A blaze which filled the land,

Galloping over the tree tops
  Like scouts a mile ahead,
Of the footless army of ruin—
  Till the life of a province had fled.

Again the homestead rises,
  And horned beasts crop the grass,
The damper and the smoking tea
  Are free to all that pass.
Then the earth is torn, and the curse has come,
  Which was cursed in the days of old,
For hell never fashioned a fouler thing
  Than a crop of unearnèd gold.
Till men are grubs, and the hounds of hate
  Are spawned from the greedy mud,
And they shelter beneath my friendly boughs
  The robbers which thrive on blood.

What matted beards and shaggy,
  What garments stained with drink,
What oaths and filthy curses
  Rise from that thievish sink.

    *   *   *   *   *

The gold dust spilled in sharing,
  Hounds on the robber's track ;
What flights through the thicking twilight
  Horsed on a nobler back.

Blood on the squatter's threshold,
  Blood where the mail roads bend,
Then justice, slow but certain,
  Shots! Curses! Cries! The end.

Such were the throes I witnessed,
  I saw a people rise,
I heard the shriek of engine,
  The hum of wired lies.
The town now pressed around me,
  Then came a day of dread,
The axe descended, cleft my roots,
  The forest king was dead.

But my heart was shaped in honor,
  It was made the twin of renown,
For I am the staff of the standard
  Which floats in Sydney town.
When first my colors fluttered
  All Sydney stood arrayed,
To greet the stout eight hundred
  Marching to Gordon's aid ;
Hear it, ye elder people !
  Write it with virgin pen,
The youth of a nation in armor
  To rescue the helper of men.

I shall see a millioned city—
  Thou London of the South—
Ere I pass with the lyre-bird and emu,
  Ere I pass with the flame and the drouth.
But now in the fresh, sweet breezes,
  Fair as our bay of renown,
I bear the standard of Empire,
  Which floats o'er Sydney town.

PURGATORY

TWO knights, sore battered from a hard-fought
    field,
    Muddy, hair-matted, damp with sweat and blood;
A pure fleshed bride, a lily, waited each.
The first, from horse leaped down; love-seized his
    bride,
Bruising her sore with clasp that soiled her robe
And snarled her golden hair with smear of blood,
Then dropped his head upon her lap and slept.

The other doffed the garb of loathsome war,
Then bathed and sought the rage of war to cool;
Love-torn he prayed, and then in linen slept,
Nor would approach his virgin-peace while taint
Of that foul war on garb or soul remained.
Next morn, 'mid beauty's order they embraced
As though a strong red rose a jonquil kissed.

THE SONG OF A VIGNETTE

PLEASANT are palace, power and place,
Ambition has its ardent stinging ;
But Love's the fire which warms our race.

Let Swift on cynic pages trace,
" Gold sets all marriage-bells a-ringing
" Pleasant are palace, power and place."

I'll fondly dream of Flora's grace,
'Tis action sets our skiff a-swinging ;
But Love's the fire which warms our race.

The ancient earl rides down his chase,
To our young lips the words leap springing,
" Pleasant are palace, power and place."

His sad, old eyes look into space,
He sighs, "I'm great beyond men's singing,
" But Love's the fire which warms our race."

Then let us kiss, oh, fond, fair face,
With love we'll prove through tender clinging,
Pleasant are palace, power, and place ;
But Love's the fire which warms our race.

SOPHOCLES TRIUMPHANT

In his old age, Sophocles was charged by his son, Iophon, with dotage and incapacity to conduct his family affairs. He gained a favorable decision from his judges by reciting a portion of a newly-finished tragedy, entitled Achilles.

OLD man, gray, reverend son of Sophilus,
    Approach ! The gods themselves have called
      thee friend,
Unbarred the harvest of their golden grain.
And thou hast reaped until the years have weighed thy
    sickled hand.
Draw near and listen to thy son's deep prayer.
But now thy Iophon petitions loud,
Swearing before the altar of the gods,
And makes report concerning thee, his sire,
As a rich city whose safe-keeping walls,
Now breached by time, admit the hungry foe.
His blood demands a portion of thy stores.
The amber honey of the busy hive
Is for the queen bee's nourishment : Not less
Is the queen guarded, or she breaks away,
And scatters all the swarm. So lest thou err,
And thy transgressions fall on other heads,
It is for us, who regulate the State,
To sift this close affair, oh ! Sophocles ;

For, without judgment, age and suckling babe
Are like.   What sayest thou?   Let thy answer weigh
Against the accusation.   Old man, speak!

Sophocles

Oh, puissant judges, it is yours to speak,
Mine to obey.   Heed not my trembling limbs,
Nor crawling words, nor anger's blunted edge,
Nor the dull frosty eye.   Behold, the gods
Balance with wisdom all these cureless ills.
And yet, in truth, my heavy eyes both seek
And fear the light; the tripping maids of hope
No longer deck my dwindling day with wreaths!
But hang dull aches upon each added year.
Oh, triple curse! to feel my thin white hair
Stirred by the hungry breath of anxious youth;
Before I tread lone night, to be alone,
To stand upon the threshold of the dark,
While mine own flesh shrieks through the halls of peace,
Before the sun goes down the darkling way
A flight of rays it sends, as full and fair
As ever volleyed in the train of dawn.—
And night or morn, we hymn, the self-same sun,
Hear me, O muses, with your quiring tread,
O, sweetest maidens, memory's daughters hear,
I, who have bathed your feet with lavish verse,
Teach men, I pray, to anguish for the song,
And for the ancient singer, Sophocles.

" Achilles "

Chorus of Grecian Virgins

Never more to see the grain
  Ripple o'er the Grecian plain,
Nor to taste the dulcet cup,
  Nor the tepid milk to sup.
No more bleaching of the gown,
  No more wearing of the crown.
Never more in sacred glades,
  'Tween the lines of blushing maids,
Like a bending rose to spin,
  While their white arms arch thee in.
Never more the incensed hymns,
  Braided hair and washéd limbs.
When the joy-crammed day has fled,
  Sinking on the well-piled bed.
Blindly blows the wind of pain,
  Tangles up the virgin skein,
Drives it, soft and pale with fears,
  Thwart the cutting of the shears.

Iphigenia

'Tis the hillock, the place. Now arm me with spear,
    and let this array
See monarch and youth and frosty-veined sage face
    Iphigenia to slay.

O, ye girl-slaying Greeks! The shame of my doom
    shall blow like a seed
O'er the dear Grecian homes, and murder shall spring
    like a poisonous weed.
'Gainst a woman you war, a woman you'd make the
    slave of your pains.
Ye kings, wear like Hercules Omphale's dress! O,
    spearsmen, be cranes!
Shed armor and sword; for a battle is on, a virgin is
    gored!
Have the gods then forgot the altars I decked, the liba-
    tions I poured?
I am death-smitten twice. In battle or plague men
    hope till they die;
But death is derision, a sacrilege foul, when the pulses
    beat high.
Ye are women, I'm man, I will cry to the gods. I will
    shriek 'mid your songs!
Force me down, rag my robes, and fell me with blows
    and bind me with thongs,
'Till the altar is fouled and the God is blasphemed, 'till
    the clay and blood mix,
And, untimely, I fleet and wander for aye by the ghost-
    haunted Styx.

Chorus of Grecian Virgins

Daughter of a king, be sage,
Piece not life with impious rage,
From the gods are joy and ache,
Theirs to give and theirs to take.
Pause, reflect, endure thy state,
No one flees the grip of fate,
And its righteous-working will
Some it takes from greater ill,
Some, because in years long sped,
By their blood the good have bled,
Yield thee, then, and silent bleed,
If thy dying is decreed,
Then the forfeit must be paid,
Pestilence or honor's blade
Dying, let thy blessing stay,
Daughter of a king, obey !

Iphigenia

Ah ! where is the youth, that splendid betrothed my
ripe years demand ?
I am robbed of a husband, bereaved of a son to inherit
the land.
Shall you cling to your wives in fondest delight, and
deny me that bliss ?
Shall you long for your children, and kiss them in
dream, and forbid me that kiss ?

Yea, the ancient man lives in the deeds of his son and
    kindleth then
With the flaming of youth.   I ne'er shall be crowned
    the mother of men.
Nay, pluck me not down, for anger has ebbed, and
    submissive I bow
To the alterless fates.   I will blot out your wiles with
    the gift of a vow.
Be entreated, pure huntress, receive this one life and
    let the Greeks live ;
Shine thou on their prows, and breathe on their sails,
    and prosperity give
That each king may return to his dear one, and babe,
    and deep-cherished strand,
That my sire may reign in the great palace-hall of the
    Argian land.
Lo ! the goddess replies.   Through the thicket there
    flees a milky-white hind,
Fierce anger, dumb anguish have fallen away, and with
    firm, constant mind,
On the altar of Dian, arrayed as her bride, a virgin
    I lie,
At the will of the gods, for country and sire, all patient,
    I die !

Chorus of Grecian Maidens

Woe for her untimely sped,
Banished from the nuptial bed,
Ah ! she boats the dreadful wave,
Finds no children in the grave,
Sees no cradled infant lie,
Rosebud mouth and eager eye,
Hands and feet which never rest,
Till he find her aching breast,
Then, when milking joys are gone,
He shall make his first step on,
Cross the room, oh, dreadful road,
Till he find her, love's abode,
Woe for her, a barren tree,
Blasted in virginity !

As when the winter's sun flames sudden forth,
Kissing the glassy plain and candied trees,
The icicles flash clapping to the ground,
So with a mighty beating of their hands,
Th' exulting people thundered "Sophocles."

THE VULTURE'S TRYST

A studio of Munich, that city Art calls "mine"—
How the heedless sunbeams shine
On splashes of color, casts of clay,
On an antique shield from a Grecian fray.
Skins of the leopard, tapestry old,
Scarlet fur-collared and crowned with gold.
There's a picture hung on the studio wall,
Compelling the glances and wonder of all.
Description lacks outline, and language lacks blaze,
Yet this is the picture to him who will gaze:

The Picture

From behind an effect of light comes through
The pavilion stuff, with its striped red and blue,
Whose open and upper flap shows the sky.
Back to the left of this marquee lie
Chariot wheels, heaps of ornaments old,
By the ancients fashioned in soft, dull gold.
Centre and raised, neck and shoulders bare,
Exalted and joyous, timbrel in air,
In fleecy white, on the arms gold bands,
A glowing, magnificent Jewess stands—
A richness of beauty, unworn by the brain,
And Miriam strikes the loud timbrel again.
Stands another woman far to the right,
Who has entered in beauty and brought in the light,

Which flashes across the central place,
Lighting the Hebrew's breast and face,
And the other woman has eyes of blue,
Hair of a chestnut-squirrel hue.
Over one shoulder a crimson shawl,
And the blue yachting dress shows her slender and
    tall.
The painter who paints the Hebrew in white,
Has turned at the rush of intrusive light—
With a certain bold anger, has lifted his eyes,
In his shoulders and back are emotioned surprise.

This is the painting ! bold color and plan ;
Now gaze at the painter ; rejoice if you can.
On a couch 'neath the picture, a couch linen-spread,
With his stilled face uncovered, the painter lies
    dead,
And a girl of the Hebrews beseeches his eyes,
And watches and bends o'er the dead man, who lies
With a look of contentment, lips ceasing to bind,
And the forehead off guard can afford to be kind.
O ! that smile ! as if soul overjoyed at Heaven's sight.
Had let its smile linger !   The face, not too white,
Bore the look of a child, and a sweet, tranquil glow,
'Twas pleasant and comely—it ne'er had been so ;
The ill-limping present had vanished away,
And the brightness returned, and the hope of youth's
    day.

When the nerves are starting, and brain is weak,
The click of the woodwork comes like a shriek.
There are steps ! She covers his face. With a frown
Behind the lay figure crouches down,
Where the blue and red draperies make a gloom.
Three, men with hushed voices, enter the room :
The first man, of canvas and paints has a mart.
He buys, and depreciates, pictures and art ;
Blank canvas is costly, when glorified, cheap ;
One man is his jackal ; the last man, a sheep,
An uncle, in haste to sell every stick,
And bury the dead—time belongs to the quick.
" Hm !" says the old werewolf, " in lieu of my bill,
" I will take the large painting—the dead man lies still—
" Let an artist set value ; so, Herman, be fair,"
And presto ! the jackal is ready to tear.

           " Hm ! ha ! that red bit to the right
              " A *tour de force*, yet clever ;
           " But that confusion of the lights
              " Queer art, and nature never.
           " The women, statues painted in
              " Fine, classic lines no doubt,
           " The model's face is spirited,
              " Hm ! what's it all about?
           " That bit of sky is fanciful,
              " That shadow is not bad.
           " I never saw such tint effects,
              " Such lights, the man is mad !

"The model's a patchwork, has borrowed her charms,
"Her neck from one beauty, from one, breast and arms;
"Her face, too, is copied—" There came a fierce cry.
A woman leaped forward and shrieked out, "You lie!"
'Twas the girl of the picture, in rich, splendid youth.
It has happened, will happen; lie crouching to truth.

A moment she faces chagrin and surprise,
A moment, then tear-drops are thronging her eyes;
She looks at the dead, as if loving were sin;
The door thunders open, and vigor comes in.

Second Part

A bearded face, a heavy brow; the cunning bipeds
    quailed
Before raised finger. 'Twas a bolt—as thus and thus he
    railed:
"I've listened at the door, heard through the crack;
"Like a passion-play truth enters, and drives the devils
    back;
"I'm the means by which truth works its miracles
    to-day—
"Would God had given vital breath a moment to that
    clay!
"And your lecture on the art (man shows sure descent
    from worms),
"The art of blacking colors with the glib-deceit of
    terms;

" The art of drilling heroes and keeping them in ranks ;

" Pot-boilers' chief, and dodgers' prince, your lecture
    has my thanks.

" The thought's intolerable, that one untaught in schools

" Should far surpass the jargoners, and practicers of
    rules,

" And that a something born within, combined with
    soul and heart,

" Should equal lapis-buying, and knowledge of an art.

" I point ye, ye conspirators ! ye pedagogues in fine ;

" Regular schools of thought, and art, of gesture, siege
    and spine.

" Let all men learn your shibboleth, or let them hold
    their peace—

" When God is done away with, then the genius will cease.

" Oh, yes, I'm Michael Urbenhoff—

" And at your nature-cant I scoff ;

" For I command in colors, and they obey as well :

" The gods you love approve me ! Oh, ho ! my paint-
    ings sell.

" And nature's limitation, blind force shall never bind

" My brush from splashing color, I judge by eye and
    mind.

" And I know deep-nature better than you know your
    lady's brow,

" Do you think (I've painted seraphs) that you can
    paint a cow ?

" Must I paint Heaven, which surpasses all that vision
e'er has seen,

" From studies made at Venice, in Prussian blue and
green ?

" You know a tree?   You, doubtless, know the lines
which bound a tree ;

" I know the oak-leaf's angle, and the beech's mystery.

" You've listened to my overture, now note that painting there.

" A thought is in that painting, is in it everywhere.

" For painting's something mental ; and mark, more-
over, here,

" How the lesser shapes which circle the one emotion's
sphere

" Are all subdued to nourish it !   Ye painters !   have
you eyes ?

" I do not know its title, but it should be ' Surprise,'

" Caught, and forever painted there ;

" Surprise is in its shadow, and in its light and air ;

" In the half-nude Hebrew beauty, in the high-born
lady dressed

" (My child, he was a painter, be cheered, he loved
you best).

" You do not like his painting, you, Sir Dodger !   who
can show

" Beer foaming in a tankard where the foam from top
we blow,

" And the rest is just Tomasso, who makes a fine dis-
    play,
" In his polished, mock-steel armor, just two florins
    more a day ;
" Yet the artist of that painting, paints soft down and
    subtle smile.
" Look ! that artist's coat is velvet, you can puff, and
    blow the pile,
" And in gazing on the artist, you'll discover, if you've
    eyes,
" How a back, by straining muscles, can express the
    heart's surprise.

" One word, before we sunder, and you give tongue to
    abuse,
" You did your best in smirching, notwithstanding
    you're of use—
" For God's a sovereign etcher, and man's blots and
    scratches still
" Work his etching of perfection ; 'spite yourselves,
    you do his will.
" And the fame of him, whose spirit once informed
    that icy clay
" (Ye have shaped his crown of arthood, ye have writ-
    ten down his day),
" Shall be a name of magic, so long as earth is earth,
" And grow, till fancied promise overtops existing
    worth.

" Aye, higher than his merit shall arise the critic shout,

" And the smear made by his cat's tail, shall be called fine art, no doubt.

" Be off, ye talky creatures! ye things of clique and fee !

" Leave the dead to her devotion, leave his fame to truth and me."

AT THE BACK OF THE SPHINX

SAND, nothing but sand,
 Sliding, slipping each way,
Sand, ploughing through sand,
 Longing for yesterday ;
Longing for stunted bush,
 Longing for withered grass.
Ah ! the print of the camel's foot
 Is gone, as the riders pass ;
Better the former rock,
 Better the robber-band,
Better the heated blast
 Swirling up pillars of sand.
Heat in my voiceless throat,
 Heat on my bridle hand,
Better I fancy, is death,
 Than this Sabbath of pulseless sand.
Dead is the level plain,
 Dead is the lifeless air,
Dead, all dead, but the sun,
 With the face of his fury bare.
Toiling, toiling in heat,
 Toiling, toiling in pain,
In the hope of an English weed,
 In the thought of an English rain.

I rave shut in by the heat,
 There never was water or land,
Nothing but stumble and ache,
 Nothing but anguish and sand ;
Nothing but nothing itself.
 I float in a liquid blaze,
Heat and aching and sand,
 Heat and anguish and craze.
The camels have ceased to groan,
 They die,—or they scent the green.
My guide has pointed his hand,
 I see that his eyes have seen ;
His sight is caressing the grass,
 A well, but I see a blank.
I see a speck, but his strong sight tells
 An Arab, and knows his rank :
I live in the faith of his eyes,
 At sunset 'twas mine to see,
To live by the gurgling brook,
 And to pluck ripe figs from the tree.

The Merchant's Tale

" There is one God (One righteousness,
 " One perfectness ! All hail !)
" Begetting, nor begotten. He
 " Whose mercies never fail !
" My children, Allah give you peace ;
 " Obey the holy rule."

Joy ! I shall see our Mecca shine
    White as the Prophet's mule :
Thrice joy, for I shall hear again
    Muezzin's " Allah-hu !"
With every step on holy soil,
    The Giaour fades from my view.
Those English, red with juice of grape,
    The French who Algiers rend ;
The Greek, our Islam's hated foe ;
    Yet happy be their end.
The human being sacred is
    What e'er his faith may be :
(This thought from Moslem's oasis
    Springs like a fountain free).

" Respect the man, respect his home,
    " His honor and his beast,
" Respect the place he holds as blessed,
    " His churches and his priest.
" And when ye war, first offer peace,
    " Then kill a foe ye may ;
" But if he fall, and mercy seek,
    " Ye shall not turn away.
" 'Twas Abram drave our wild sire forth
    " To roam o'er deserts lone,
" And from wayfarers take the spoil :
    " The plains are all our own ;

" God to the Arab four gifts gave,
 " The tent instead of hall ;
" Turban for crown, and verse for laws ;
 " The sword, not moated wall.
" The horsemen of a mighty foe
 " Have borne away no spoil ;
" The foot of conquest never pressed
 " Arabia's sacred soil.
" Europe her gold and silver sends,
 " And bears away our best,
" For all the treasure of the world
 " Is garnered in the West.
" But I had rather eat dried dates
 " Than Frankish sugared things ;
" I'd rather drink of Zemzem's flow
 " Than England's crystal springs ;
" And I (by fig and olive !) swear
 " There is no place on earth
" Like fruit-environèd Sana,
 " The city of my birth.

" We've many wives, but harlots few,
 " (The sun has many stars :)
" But brutes ye call us ! Christians ask
 " The hero-soul of Kars :
" Hungary's lion, Christian, knows
 " (He bowed at Mecca's shrine)
" No Arab breaks his mercy pledge,
 " That grace ye call divine.

" A curse on fickle Albion,
    " She helps to drive us forth
" Before that mad and drunken thing,
    " The savage of the North.

" I saw their city London, vast,
    " Bazaars 'neath weeping skies,
" Men packed like dates, no troops of dogs,
    " Save dogs in Christian guise.
" A place I found in London's heart,
    " Where lamps in thousands blaze,
" And painted, like Aleppo's slaves,
    " Bold women throng the ways ;
" With face and breast as fair as when
    " The eunuchs guarding stand.
" Yet say the English, woman is
    " Adored in all that land.

" 'Twas there I met her, Esther named,
    " And truly know I this,
" She's in Mohammed's bosom now
    " With pure Abdalazis.
" Her face was bare, unlike the rest
    " Her breast was hid from sight,
" Her voice like tinkling camel's bell,
    " Which softly sounds at night.
" And so she lay within my arms ;
    " I loved her as my life,
" She was the attar of all bliss,
    " She had become my wife.

" One night I sought my tent, my home,
 " The green date-palm was dead :
" My tent was empty, from its grove
 " The nightingale had fled.
" A minister, a Christian dog,
 " Had frighted Esther forth ;
" Upon our bed a note was laid,
 " I cursed the cruel North.
" I broke the seal : fell glossy hair,
 " Bound by a ribbon shred,
" Black as Mohammed's holy stone :
 " I knew the maid was dead."
  * * * * *
" She lay beside their murky stream,
 " Where Eblis ink had spilt,
" In shade of massy London Bridge
 " By genii stout built,
" With large black eyes (like houri's) dim,
 " While gazers stood about ;
" I threw my scarf across her face
 " And shut the Giaours all out.
" I tore my hair, and beat my breast,
 " I wailed, she did not stir :
" For talisman of Solomon
 " I had not bartered her.
" I felt a blast like simoon's breath,
 " My eyes were wet with dew :
" I took her cold wet hand in mine ;
 " The black scene fell from view.

" The Giaours mocked at my falling tears,
" They held me as the beasts.
" (When Jesus slays the Deggial,
" What of these dogs of priests ?)
" There is one God ! All merciful !
" Although I kiss the dust,
" Mohammed is his Prophet true !
" Kismet ! What must be, must."

PRIDE OR LOVE

A single league from Seville lie domains,
    A dukedom, scarce diminished in Time's race,
With rock-rich furlongs, realms of fruit, fat plains,
    And peasants, proudly grumbling of " His Grace."
    The third Duke wooed Gertrudis,—oh, her face !
Our Lady's, rustic-latticed !—made her wife.
    War snatched the secret suitor ; whispers base
Beat down the lilied maid.   Back from the strife
Came Duke : her Duchesshood cut sneering with a
    knife.

The Duke forgave ?   The Duke forgot ?   Perhaps.
    Patience and pride both personate disdain ;
But from the day of dancing bells, tossed caps,
    The churls ne'er saw that bride.   Men trod their
        grain,
    Scized on their pleasaunce-ground, their fount-
        cooled plain,
Called from its central dip the magic bowl,
    And built up battlements ; a massy chain
Of banishment quite hid that blissful whole :
There Duke and Duchess dwelt, with soul contenting
    soul.

Yet rumor whispered what the walls concealed :
    How workmen came at dawn—ere Prime were
      gone—
And toiled in silence ; for the sun revealed
    Nor weed, nor wilted bloom. The same sun shone
    On outer walls which put no ivy on.
No orange-bough might top their prison ledge.
    A logging door slid back for Duke and Don ;
But turned a bare, grim face on Monterege :
At the wall's foot, grass died; wall's shadow had an edge.

When came the April call of love and balm,
    Of life in bergamot and jasmine scent,
Life in banana tree and tufted palm,
    Life in the oleander, blossom bent,
    Of life at founts, where love and beauty tent,
Life in all lands ; but life intensely here,
    In floating doves, no longer winter pent,
In orange-groves, with children shrilling clear :
At morn some infant Cid to the hard wall comes near,

Leans with soft curves against the brutal gates,
    Fingers the mortar, gripping mass to mass—
As hate joins tyrants when they menace states.
    The grudging wicket gapes, the workmen pass
    Out from sweet joy, across the shade-killed grass ;
And the boy sees, in brief, delicious doze,
    Statues and bloomage, in a spring-bossed mass,
Terrace o'er terrace, every flower which grows.
There—but he sees it not—beauty beleaguered rose.

With dancer's leap, a palace poised in air,
    Not snow, not ivory, not foam of tide ;
But jets of living song arrested there ;
    Pale moonlight, stitched with snow, wooed to abide
    By tender sympathy, not massive pride,
And rest for aye on Nature's blossomed lap.
    The awning front was frostwork petrified,
Whose poles were spear-shafts, each with scalloped cap,
Whose poles were tulips slight, a wind had made them snap.

O'er open doorway sprang with rainbow grace
    A wide, jambed arch, a leaf and scroll array,
A magic needle-work, a dream in lace.
    Within the house touch fashioned plastic clay
    To fair snow crystals, curves, and frozen spray.
'Neath feet, enameled tiles wore fadeless dyes ;
    There shone the Moorish blue, now lost for aye—
These tiles showed naught of man to conjure sighs,
But circles, scrolls, and stars; ferns, birds, and butterflies.

The court of rest, rest, save the clouds above,
    Through halls of lily-heads in flight you find ;
This was the heart and centre-space, of love.
    The water-tank was blue, walls undefined,
    A gray which had some rosy warmth behind ;
Fern-scrolls and feather-scrolls filled all the space—
    An ease, as if some grace-creating mind
Had broidered veils of dreaming o'er the place—
And here forever dwelt beauty, and love and grace.

Her Room

Cardinal hangings flaked with gold,
Purer silk from the loom ne'er roll'd,
Every niche of the dainty room
Had its orange-trees frothed with bloom.
Like bees of Eden, poised for flight,
Space above gave the chamber light.
As pearly rain makes blossoms bright,
With gems he feeds her tender sight.
Green as gold-leaf when sun shines through,
Or diamonds, with souls of blue,
Or sapphires from the Orient—
Moonlight, concentred, never spent :
Gems, whose slight settings seemed to float,
Of flame 'neath smoke, flame not remote :
Against white necks such opals glow,
Like signal-fires across the snow.

And soft the velvet walks they trod ;
She was his own, he was her god :
She longed to him, all-loving wise ;
Her beauty fed his haughty eyes.
"Ask what you will, sweetheart," he'd say,
" Those village clods shall rue the day
" They puffed their scorn against my doe.
" Churls ! Sweet ! the palace you shall know ;
" The kin who caused your tears to flow,
" Now weed your walks, shall be more low :

" The fabric of your robe, fair dear,
" Shall dower their daughters half a year.
" Your shoes shall buy their richest clown ;
" Around your neck shall shine the town !
" Cling, cling, my love, in mingled life,
" And tremble not !   You're mine ; my wife.
" A year, and who shall doubt your race ?
" The sunburn leaves the bronze-smooth face ;
" Your walk shall grow a stately glide ;
" Your curtsy have its touch of pride.
" Be beautiful ! and let them see
" Your kiss is worth a monarch's fee.
" Be beautiful ! this is thy life :
" With grace blot out the peasant wife."

From autumn's red to spring-time's pearl,
Alone, save some cold island earl,
Or prince of some complacent race,
Or her Duke's kin, by her Duke's grace.
One morn she rose with day's first beam ;
He slept and murmured in a dream,
And called his war-cry, waved his hand,
Babbled of councils and command.

Adown the stairs she went, rich clad,
So white, so still, so cold, so sad.
Behind her eyelids tear-drops pressed,
She longed for something unexpressed.

For "Oh," she said, and paused a space,
" I'm weary of this ordered place.
" Beauty by sameness quenched ; I wis
" What oped in passion, ends in this,
" In this !   I see the people pass,
" As a sick child, through colored glass."
Just then, with cry, and croon, and cheer,
She heard a mother singing near,
A babe's voice, thing forbidden, rang ;
And soft the nursing mother sang :

Song

Good St. Clement keep thy soul,
   When thou goest to sea.
Good St. Peter guide thy sword,
   When in war thou be.
Good St. Patrick guard thy foot
   From the wolf and snake.
Good St. Luke, oh, cure my babe,
   For sweet Jesu's sake !
Lady Mary guard thy breast,
   Good St. John likewise ;
Make my baby sweet and strong,
   Make my baby wise.
Oh, drink, my babe, and never fear !
The saints are all around thee here.

" Her babe ! " Gertrudis said, " and I
" Am weary of the earth and sky.
" This is my nothing, that, her all."
The Duchess turned and climbed the wall,
And on its rough and barren ledge
She leant and looked to Monterege.
She conjured up each peasant face,
She saw them in the market-place,
The muleteers came clacking by,
She heard the water carriers' cry,
She saw the gossips by the fount,
The children played, the men made count
Of when the purpling grapes would cling,
What olives should October bring ;
And would the gypsies come this year ?
Would mules be scarce and horses dear ?

The Duchess woke, she turned, she sighed,
But in the waking, comfort died.

THE RAMSAY LANES
To T. B.

I owned Aladdin's lamp one fortunate day,
Controlled a greater spirit than myself,
A soul whose benefactions made him mine,
One who thought " good " a better word than " great ;"
For they were great things which he threw behind,
When he left England for the love of Mann.
A name large writ on Oxford's ancient roll,
That gift of tongues, which makes the critic's pen
Great as the marshal's staff.   All these he dropped
With careless unreluctance ; quite content
To be the island's heart and sing its songs,
Content to know the Manxman and his isle,
As dogs know masters, or a priest his mass.
And he was wise to drop the scholar's robe.
The moth which flames in splendor 'thwart the sun
Becomes at rest-time part of Nature's gray.
These were the fringes of his 'quaintanceship ;
For Nature was a thing so much beloved,
That he could pass dumb, restful hours with her,
Like lovers glad to breathe a neighbored air.
And part of this he taught me on the day
I reveled in his ripe felicity.
He taught me flowers and peaks were something more
Than scented nosegays and lookouts for man.

I'd gone to Nature in my 'prentice days,
And felt the blind delight of every sense;
But now began rest, satisfaction, peace.
And so I cry with that blind man of yore,
" I know not how the miracle was done,
" But I was blind, and now, indeed, I see."

In Nature's Byways

Near an old bowling green, by elder ringed,
Nature and I changed hearts.
                                   I knew it first,
Watching the wrens.   One gold-crowned flutterer,
Frankly familiar, feasted from my hand.
And next I met a pair of chaffinches,
And they, too, knew that I had sylvan grown.
Aye, e'en the hen, with eggs and hopes alert,
Allowed me, bending pithy twigs aside,
To peep within her nest, and never stirred,
But tarried, couched in matronly content.
Thus Nature's freedom was conferred on me,
The right to share in all the joy of growth,
To turn the pages of the hours, and read
The sunset epics and the buds of prayer.
And yet, to speak the truth, for months I went,
Calling the kingcups, buttercups, no doubt;
Till love of field and woodland grew apace,
And sight and knowledge sauntered hand in hand.

This happed last summer.   Summer comes again.
Down perfumed winds there floats a gauzy clew,
Which leads me on through mazy labyrinths
Of solitude to Nature's hidden things—
Unworded essences, deep felt at dusk :
A state you'll understand, if you perceive
How affable the scent of pansy is.
On through the varied green that clew has led,
To where my mistress, Nature's self, abides.
Through summer nights, there might I sleep unscathed.
The hare would cuddle close, the fairies chime :
He's one of us, he's wet with flower-dew,
And 'round him floats the scent of broken fern.

July, I greet you ! Exquisite July !
From the half-grudging clanship of the birds—
Allowed, I seek the gipsy fellowship ;
And, as the pulsing sap puts forth the flower,
So, warmed by scent and beauty, I must sing :

A Song for the Land

Here fancy first dwelt, and they crowned her with
    thyme,
And hymned her with waterfalls, primitive rhyme.
Dear, motionful Goddess, endow me with might,
While I sing Ellen Vannin, the Isle of Delight :
By that grace where thy fern droops to talk to the rills ;
By thy freshness that blows o'er thy purple-clad hills ;

By thy sweetness which tempts us to couch on the sod ;
By thy gorse like the burn-bush, where Moses saw
    God ;
By thy peaks, where a giant is dwarfed to a bird ;
By thy glens, where the kiss of the lover is heard ;
By all that is fragrant, and restful and free,
I greet thee, oh island ! Oh, sweet Ben My-Chree.
I greet thy dear lanes where the nesting bird cheeps,
Where behind drooped laburnum the cottage boy
    peeps.
Full oft have I turned from the surf's thunder-ledge,
To recreate soul by the bloom-matted hedge.
Again do I walk with thick branches o'erhead,
Like the aisle of St. German, but living, not dead ;
And passing from coolness, from mimic of night,
I come to the hedges, alert in the light,
Where wonders of perfume and color are blent :
There's woodbine, which conquers the brine with its
    scent,
And here came the sea-foam, and found an abode ;
It lives in the trammon, which bushes the road.
This bindweed outchaliced when morning arose,
For faint through its whiteness the morning-star
    shows ;
And here where the thorn-bush and brier unite,
The dog-rose has ventured, pink, perfumed and slight.
The thorn will not rend her, though me it oft rends,
For here, in the greenery, all things are friends.

The Gipsy Camp

Beyond the solid, yellow, prickling gorse,
Is pitched, with garish taste, a Gipsy camp.
The sky is blue, nay, purple, to my ken,
Purple as when hands press on eyelids closed.

There Bucklee, monarch of the moors, is housed.
A scampish knave, free nature's Bedouin,
Whose lies are marvels of imaginings,
And whose experience o'ertops his lies.

Long e're I reach the camp, the man is seen:
The free mouth guarded by the watchful eyes,
Not e'en a white hair in his ample beard,
His easy garb without a speck of dirt.
In cautious sloth he poises 'gainst a thorn,
Playing a zither, nursed upon his knee,
And as he yawns, reveals a flash of white.

As I approached, he smiled and greeted me
In Romany, which I, henceforth, translate.
His suavity had nothing of surprise.
A knave he was, who ciphered while he laughed;
You felt the lynx beneath his tricksy smile:
He'd shoe a horse, his hammer keeping tune,
Then cheaply sell the beast he'd never owned.

The foreign, flashing scene ! Un-English were
The ragged, romping boys and dark-locked girls,
With conscious smiles of honest vanity.
A sight as gorgeous as to mount a hill,
And see the sun's red ball lie on its top.

With broadcast greetings 'round, I made my way
Within the inner tents, and, ere I sat,
Made first my brief obeisance to the crane,
Who, like an evil toad, crouched o'er the blaze,
And counted life by warmth and scent of food ;
Then claimed the tale, since May-tide, pledged to me,
And in the pauses of blithe Bucklee's words,
I let my gaze fly out a little space
To bathe itself in beauty all aglow :
For near, by tenting etiquette, was placed,
Zuba, the poppy-flushed and jewel-eyed.

Bucklee's Tale

My brother, God upon you rest ;
    Your wish I will not balk,
You helped me in the prison-cell,
    And Romany can talk.

A hundred hundred years we've taught
    Our Gipsy girls to trade
In all things but their honor—yet
    Trainette the wanton played.

"Begone," we cried, "foul, tainted thing
    From camp and kettle go:
His chain of coins is round your neck,
    Go with your Gorgio."

So, from the tent we thrust Trainette,
    And cast her from our race:
We laughed, and cried, and sang, but ne'er
    At cross-roads left a trace.

When she fell sick, he cast her off
    Without a single pang:
The news soon reached our ears, and loud
    Our bitter curses rang.

She wandered far in search of us;
    The brooks were swelled with snow,
The river took her at the ford—
    We swore to lay him low.

Next night we drowed his pigs and sheep,
    And then he fled afar.
Our curses followed on the air,
    Like sparks from hammered bar.

At length one year we reached the Isle,
    As is our Gipsy plan—
Baked one June in the Isle of Wight,
    Next June revived in Man.

The girls told fortunes—philtres sold,
  The men boxed in the ring,
For food we broiled hedgehogs, or hares,
  Or any picked-up thing.

One dusky night our Queen Matskeal
  (Who then was with the bands)
Spied out the carle, in whose bad blood
  We'd sworn to wash our hands.

The hound had lost his cursèd gold,
  His ugly face was pale,
A hunted look was in his eyes ;
  He drove the midnight Mail.

I like the Isle, its herbs and lanes,
  Its wakes and cattle fairs,
Its wastes of furze—a royal camp
  And covert for the hares.

In such a brake, behind the hedge,
  We waited for his tread :
By "we," I mean the Queen, myself,
  And Penhurst, lately dead.

We heard the Mail roar down the hill ;
  Then at its foot grow dumb,
To roar again with jog of hoof
  As on we heard it come.

From the left hedge, then Penhurst leaped,
　　And on the Mail-step sprang—
He backward fell, the snapping step
　　Like ping of bullet rang.

But I, from out the right-hand hedge,
　　Jumped forward with a bound,
And close embraced the driver's neck,
　　And dragged him to the ground.

The Mail without a driver went
　　On its accustomed way,
The horse unhurt, the bags untouched :
　　The Gipsies had their prey.

We trailed the brute across two fields,
　　In haste to end the strife,
And threw him headlong in the stream,
　　To let it drink his life.

We hauled him forth to lay him down
　　Upon a ledge of stone,
Where cold and dying, he might see
　　The Gipsies had their own.

And as he slowly ope'd his eyes,
　　We cursed our broken plan :
The black-souled Gorgio had 'scaped—
　　We'd trapped another man.

Then rose the Queen and kissed him twice,
　　And as she kissed, he died.
The scheme was bravely ventured on,
　　The plan was fairly tried.

But of that hound I've nothing heard,
　　Either of woe or weal :
The wrong man died ? but then he had
　　The kiss of Queen Matskeal.

A BIBLIOGRAPHER

His book-plate

H. Asaph Gyle

*Si regna non habere possumus
Provincias tamen habere libet*

HOW lovingly Gyle touched a book,
      A mellow, ancient timer;
   Not with the curt, rough clutch of clown,
      Nor eager rush of rhymer.
The books he longed for must be rare,
      And rich in soul and manner,
Not decked in foppish gems and gold,
      In choice hides from the tanner;—
In Russia some, in vellum some,
      Some green as leaves in summer,
Citron, or ruby at the whim
      Of Hering, Payne, or Plummer

The " Lives of Flemish Painters "
      He extra-illustrated,
And fifty thousand pounds, too, went
      Ere text and print were mated :—

For many thousand artist proofs,
  Maps, letters autographic,
Etchings, and charts with aquarelles
  Of tint and tone seraphic;
Original designs were there
  By living art appended;—
Five volumes were when he began,
  Two hundred when he ended:—
All bound in matchless livery
  Both sober and resplendent,
The doublé with four hundred arms
  Of kings and states dependent:—
The book-mad cried, "Ecstatic works!"
  The vast world, "Gorgeous fooling!"
And gazed askance at crushed levant,
  And geometric tooling.

By journey of two thousand miles
  He gained (for floods not stopping)
The vellum "Spira Virgil," great
  In height, all copies topping.
He had the Magna Charta, rich
  In golden letters printed,
Four copies once, now only three
  (He burnt one, it is hinted).

Behold him, like a gentle saint—
  (On his inlaying table
The secret life of good Queen Bess,
  Found 'neath an ancient gable.)

Nose pointed, somewhat peering eyes,
   'Tween brows the judging wrinkle;
A placid face, save when a book
   Made all the visage twinkle;
Save when "editions first," "de luxe,"
   "Fifteeners" gave him gladness;
"A Grolier," I hear again
   The phrases of book-madness,
"Large Paper," "vellum," "uncut leaves,"
   "Uniques," (beyond all giving)
"Reynard the Foxe," his Caxton find,
   Lent him a lease of living.
And yet he was no one-book man
   The Caxtons ever finding;
Nor was he mad for Elzevirs,
   For vellum as a binding;
No Aldine worshipper was he
   With Dibdin for a prophet,
And though he swore by Roger Payne
   He often bound with Moffit.
He showed his treasures, handling books
   He never counted treason.
Of course, his tomes were never lent,—
   Book-charity in reason.
The "Old Book Kingdom" no one rules;
   Has never claimed to, truly;
A province (as his book-plate hints)
   He governed well and duly.

Men say he died 'mid heathen rites,
  The customed half-truth libel ;
I read to him the night he died,
  From his " Blackletter Bible."
And when I spoke of meeting friends,
  He answered somewhat oddly,
" Yes, Dibdin I should like to meet,
  " And Heber too, and Bodley."
I read from " Bits of Hindoo Books,"
  (On vellum printed rarely.
His gift because the leaves were cropped—
  Because he loved me fairly.)
The face turned marble as I read,
  His spirit went a-flitting—
These words are not our Holy words,
  Yet they had something fitting :—

From the Book of Destiny

It is set down in the Book of Destiny how from the circle of time which turns on itself, and has neither first nor last, from the womb of being, sprang two brothers, and they were Brahma, and Reason ; and as a man and his shadow they went forth on the paths of righteousness. But as shadows are wont, Reason projected itself in a reverie beyond the measured pace of Brahma ; and confused by its own darkness sent back to the fire, the winds, the circles of intellignece, and the Prince of scents and sounds, monstrous pictures of gloom, for its experience might be likened unto a man writing in his own shadow. Then Brahma from the tender depths of his eternal pity divested his presence of Reason forever ; and scattered it as the rays of the sun are scattered ; and confined each particle in dimly-lighted dwellings; dwellings whose component

*parts are the tides which shift and the clay which crumbles,
namely, in the bodies of men; but these rays still projecting into the
future, indeed permitted man neither repose nor joy—then the great
god Indra, moved by man's desolation, sought the sacred abode of
Brahma, and invoked his divine aid; and Brahma spake, saying,
—" O, Ruler of the Three Worlds, let man's sight be lessened; and
let him cease to gaze beyond the green of earth"—and hence the
proverb arose, " He who would find good, and flee gloom, must content his vision with the horizon of earth."*

MASTER FIGHT-A-FIGHT GOES TO COURT

"THE soul which sinneth, it shall die."
Who heareth our report?
The shepherd of this flock hath trod
The sin-defiles of court.
The duellist and rake are there,
The fool a-gibbering,
The wife and daughter of the great,
All louting to the King—
Divines who hear not blasphemy
When pages lewdly sing;
And maids of honor dressed to snare,
All pleasuring the King.
Prelatic Dove had preached the morn—
Ennui began to sting.
Said some one, " Let's bring Fight-a-Fight,
" And bate him 'fore the King."
" They brought me on through splendid halls,
" With lackeys in a ring;
" The page and porter throwing dice—
" So onward to the King :
" Past men, obscene, a jest with girls
" Mincing and posturing;
" 'Mid luxury no words express—
" Lights, soldiers—then the King :

" A splendid gallery all carved,

"Wax candles, music's ting,

" Heaped gold, and those who gamed for gold—

"All heedless of the King.

" The Lord's day,—yet a French boy sang

" Words with a devil sting ;

" And toying with three Jezebels,

"At last I saw the King.

" And never face more black, more sad,

" Spite song and wanton string,

" Than he who touched a Rahab's cheek,

" Than he they called the King.

" Good fellow," said he, " thou hast writ

" And preached all sins anent,

" Hast thou no word for one Charles Stuart?"

" Said I, ' O King, repent :

"Save goodness, all is vanity

" Among the sons of men ;

" It is appointed man to die,

" The judgment follows then—

" A judgment far beyond cogged dice

" Where jest and filthy song

" Shall plead no more, where truth is truth,

" And right unmasketh wrong—

" 'Gainst lewdness, lust and gluttony,

" God's judgment is arrayed."

" The King's eye flashed, the women frowned,

" Unmoved the gamesters played—

" Dumb dogs are all thy counsellors,
  " Dumb dogs thy so-called priests,
" The women here are worse than men,
  " The men below the beasts—
" Here, Charles, are nought but rotten hearts,
  " Jests hurled from Satan's sling,
" Sodom, without two righteous men
  " Is thy foul palace, King.
" Put by, thyself, put by, thy slaves,
  " Who kill thy soul; this do."
" Oddsfish," the King cried, starting up,
  " There's mercy yet for you."
Then " Treason," shrieked Dame Castlemaine,
  And swords flashed to and fro,
And all the gamesters crowded round;
  But ere they struck a blow
" Stand back, my lieges," cried King Charles,
  " Here! guard him to his door.
" Gadzooks, this chaplain of old Noll
  " Shall go in state—no more."
With guards afront and guards aback
  All gently was I thrust
Out of the gates; thank God I spake,
  For now that King is dust.

TIME'S CIRCLE WIDENS THROUGH ETERNITY

ORNING and night, at wonted time and place
You have an eye upon your mirror's face,
Notice complacent smile, and little scar,
But straight forget what sort of man you are.
A man, one night, approaches you, his pace
Familiar yet unknown, a haggard face.
You start to find a wall with mirrors glassed,
Making the hall interminably vast.
You have beheld your face without its smiles,
Vision has carried sight down ghastly aisles.

And so, in dreams, self wanders wild and free,
Without the help and snare observancy.
Then strange plants grow and weeds and noxious burrs,
Then only are we linked to all that stirs.
I know that Nature's moods defy man's spell,
The mists roll up and rust his marriage bell.
When death from frantic arms a wife has raped,
No blossom droops, the snow-drop is not craped,
And yet, raretimes, the throes of some soul sped
Have widowed earth, a-shrieking, " Pan is dead ! "
Lions grew bold and spirit-voices cried
The pregnant laboring hours ere Julius died.
Mighty the gale by which the masts are thinned,
Awful the cherubim behind the wind.

Add to the nights of joy and grief and pain,
The nights of naked nerves and wakeful brain,
The nights of self, confronted with its sins,
When here on earth the judgment day begins.
Those other nights, when spirits cram the wold,
When sudden shudders occupy the bold.
Because his soul perceives the fleshless host,
His body huddles, lest it brush a ghost.
It was my hour, I felt a boding calm,
I moved in space and heard a dirge-like psalm.
Not far was little earth with lights aswoon,
A mighty halo hooped the ancient moon.
Then as I went I felt a presence, next
I tossed my arms, stood doubtful and perplexed.
An apparition came with solemn glide ;
Between the moon and me, I felt it bide.
A chill surged up : a pleasant scent came near ;
And awe possessed me, awe, apart from fear ;
It was a shade more vibrant and more light
Than phantom leaves which dance before sick sight.
In color like th' elusive rainbowing
Which burnishes the dragon-fly's swift wing.
A flame-picked outline traced on gauze it hung ;
The dearest shape on earth when I was young.
With dream's creative instance bubbled joy,
I felt the pure, sweet rapture of a boy ;
Nor needed I to think up to a thought,
No train was flashing visions, they were brought.

Twixt flash and powder's flame the space is wide
Compared to that which found me by her side.
The mould was broken, spirit dropped its clay,
Emerged a shining core, as if sun's ray
Should coax from mud the lily, lend it wings,
So was I plucked from gross impeding things.

At once came spirit lore ; without a pause
I knew of earth-bound spirits and their laws.
I saw the end of mortals who abuse
Their highest gifts, of those who failed to use
Their utmost power at its utmost height.
I saw their penance. She was for delight
Allowed by heaven to solace me a space,
And re-baptize me to an early grace.

Two shades drew near yet dim as though afar
For through their fading gauze I saw a star
Which sparked the far horizon's lowest line.
They hung in sky uncertain and supine ;
Yet in them, little spiral whirlwind sped,
A sort of nothing-emptiness which spread
Like to that motion when the bubble shakes,
When beauty can no more, and so it breaks.
Their faces were two revelers surprised,
By savage death, two gluttons gorgonized.
Voices they had of eider-down and whey
Smooth as a gliding snake 'gainst evening's gray.

Then said the one, " I know this is my last,
" The whirl of nothingness consumes me fast.
" I may recall, to Him be all the praise !
" The sweetest moment of my wasted days."
   * * * * *
Gluttonous words of sauces, meats and wines,
Of dainty cates, liqueurs and fragrant pines,
Tuliped parterres, of gaudy, gilded rooms,
Of figures draped, pastilles and rich perfumes ;
Of every whim and bait by which earth can
Capture the epicure, and kill the man.
All this I heard ; they spent their latest sighs
On seasoned flesh, gilt clay, and flaming dyes.
Then like dust-pillars which the whirlwinds bear,
The figures brake and scattered through the air.

A woman-man came near, for it was twain
Pure jets of passion, pinion-plucked by pain.
Happy those lives where shame has gnawed no root,
And yet the hornet pierces noble fruit.
Crowned blossoms in the sheltered garden grow ;
The Edelwis is fair, despite the snow.
What cunning gyves forbade this spirit's flight ?
What fault could bind this palpitating light ?
This was the weight which clogged th' ethereal wing,
While in the flesh he did the lesser thing.
Born music's lord, its strains were never sung
Where men and angels find a mingled tongue :

He wasted self (though launched for the divine)
In songs of sugared love and poppied wine.
I saw that hope set limits to his pain,
Yet grief was there, I marked the fettered strain.

Fetters all fine and yet of giant force ;
Compared to these the spider's web was coarse ;
Fine as the silk of some resolve, but fell,
As hammered steel ; they drew him to his cell,
Within whose ancient deeps he penanced sin.
The amber bosom of a violin,
Once Paganini's frenzy found it true
And he had loved it, time had loved it too.
That time which leaves faint residues behind,
Bland as the mellow voices of the blind.
In such a bath, are dipped some violins,
Till full, pure, resonance her reign begins.

And then I knew one thing shall call down peace,
Shall break all chains and give this soul release,
One thing's return shall make this spirit whole,
That banished thing, that lack within its soul.
Those pure neglected strains have solvent power
O'er iron custom.—Then I blessed my dower ;
My table round ! Each finger was a peer,
Swift to obey the Arthur of the ear—
That ear which guarded meditations flow,
So finely tuned it heard the barley grow.

Soft as one lifts a little sleeping maid,
I took the violin, and then I played
A solemn flourish, resonant and long,
Not cold ambition, aspiration's song.
Simple and pure and ever mounting higher,
A lofty climbing up from spire to spire,
And ever up beyond the steepled sky
Above the mighty mountains, higher, high,
All's Heaven.—The sun lets down her golden shrouds
And the pale Christ sits throned upon the clouds,
Up, ever up, beyond the change of time
Into the blue and white of the sublime.
By my freed soul, I felt he broke his chains,
Deaf hell alone withstands such buoyant strains.

Now from the strings I drew a solemn prayer,
Sonorous and all warm, a Heaven-rich air;
Where aspiration ended, this began
In Beulah's plains, beyond the ken of man,
To Aiden's edge a trembling spirit clung,
While angels with a welcome round it hung,
Coaxed it with rapture sweet as God's consent,
Dissolved all fears and holy comfort lent
To the shy soul borne o'er the heavenly way,
With velvet gladness, soft but never gay.
Some sheltered it with boughs from " Eden's Tree,"
On, on, they glide with blissful purity,

Over the plains while Eden beameth near ;
Now sweet persuasion antidotes all fear,
More full the song.   I felt th' immortal leaven,
One step, like Enoch I had ravished Heaven.

With loving eye the spirit passed me by ;
Then Handel's music vanished in a sigh.
At the dim moon I stared for night had waned,
And mourned to think how Heaven was nearly gained.

A BLACK SWAN DIETH

An Author's Complaint, on the Flyleaf of
his Book, found in an Old Book-Store.

THE first that I loved was flesh and blood ;
    The mind and its psychic mist
Were in small degree, but the red blood ran
    And bloomed in the lips I kissed.
Then ardent I was, ambitious and apt,
    For the promise of youth was there.
The next was a girl like a silver sphere
    Enclosed in a crystal square ;
Yet there was promise of brightest things ;
    The ear of the world was bent
To list to my song, but the poet-thoughts
    Were thoughts that with childhood went ;
My chips of quaint learning, wanted blaze ;
    How few can rub wood till it flame,
And my book ! it was dead, on the shelves unbought,
    The critics derided my name,
And men shut me up as though in a tomb,
    I am living, and I am dead ;
And slovenly hands are thumbing my book ;
    I failed : and was left unread.
One day when chill loneliness flooded my soul,
    Long fretted by poverty's grips,
Nina, my hands in her warm hands took
    And kissed me on brow and lips.

Read this one song, I ask nothing more
   I will take it as a payment for fame.
Read, think of my hearing, my Nina, my pearl,
   I have failed ; but remember her name :—

THEY STONED STEPHEN CALLING UPON GOD

AND you would woo me to your creed,
    A realm of peace without a taint
Of doubt, for it did martyrs bleed,
    Not all the martyrs, gentle saint,
For no new road was ever built,
    But some one laid existence down.
Oft heated haste calls progress guilt;
    We know how Stephen won his crown.
We know that long discourse which taught;
    His stern reproach, which pierced each breast;
His short brief vision, glory fraught—
    Then cruel stones, sharp death and rest.

And at his name, our praise flows fast,
    Brave saint, true martyr, first to bleed;
And yet the burning words he cast
    Were 'gainst the held and reigning creed.
Against your faith, my gentle maid,
    I do not cast a single stone.
Some lambs require the shepherd's aid
    But stronger souls must walk alone.
When incense floats through chiselled aisles
    Of chapels set in garden air;
And holy chantings rise 'tween whiles,
    We wonder not at angels there.

If this were all, it were not well,
    But angels come 'neath murky skies,
They visit Peter in his cell,
    And loose his chains, and bid him rise.

Erstwhile was rent, that veil complete,
    Of faith, tradition, custom, knit—
God's glory left the Mercy Seat,
    Yet men walked on, and not unlit,
The written word was not their sun ;
    They had the light of priests and seers
That light which lighteth every one,
    Who cometh to this gift of years ;

You walk in bonds, my limbs are free ;
    You seem to see the gate of day ;
'Gainst peace and proof and pedigree,
    I put the conscience I obey.
The lowest human is a sphere,
    And Holy Ghost informs that clod ;
Beset by doubts he may not fear,
    Truth is the savor sweet to God.
A shoot will even lift a stone
    When sap of growth begins to flow,
Its right of growth who dare disown ?
    Like it, I claim my right to grow.

To you come visions of the Grail,
The still small voice, it comes to me,
You tarry near the Holy Veil,
I stand beside the inland sea.
Despite debate and angry hum
At morn or eve, which e'er is best,
I dream to every soul shall come
A sense of Christ within the breast.

ROBERT, THE GUIDE

ICTURE, before you read this simple tale,
The glistening smoothness of a precipice;
The narrow sheep-path cut across its breast,
A fenceless razor-blade, scarce two feet wide,
And halfway down, 'tween slipping foot and death,
A stunted pine, loose as an old man's tooth.

Than Robert Pearce no stouter man was known
In all Northumberland; by climbing trained
To almost miracles of eye and ear.
Curt in his seldom speech, for words seemed pain,
He'd help his talk by finger slowly swayed.
When, in his youth, his mother sought the fair,
She took with her the smooth-cheeked, chatty Tom,
And Robert wondered, in his heavy way,
Why he was left to weed, and keep the house;
Were wakes and frolics meant alone for Tom?
His manhood differed little from his youth;
He walked the streets like one in nightmare held,
Who sees some jeopardy, but cannot speak;
The women laughed at him, and cowards jeered,
Never in rage he raised his mighty arm.

His strength was at the nod and beck of all:
He was his mother's prop, his sister's stay:
The chief support of glib-tongued, idle Tom.

His sister married soon a kindly man,
And Tom talked roundly, he would marry too,
And on their blue-eyed cousin cast his eyes,
An orphan girl, who sometimes shared their meals,
The rustic beauty of the mountain side.
At fair or wake, Tom followed at her heels,
But Phoebe had her lovers by the score,
For even stolid, sheep-faced Robert brought
Her, on the chapel-days, some little gift,
A bunch of cowslips mixed with daffodils,
Or shyly left a fairing at her plate.
Why, once he plodded by her side a mile,
She with her teazing curls against his face,
He bearing all in silent sufferance.
For she, like all the rest, yerked words at him,
And with more vehemence they laughed, she raged,
He never answered her, but only looked
With great, sad eyes, and yet his hands were
    clenched,
Until the nails nigh pierced the horny palms.

Phoebe and Tom, one winter Sunday morn,
Came home from chapel, which had rocked with shouts,
Revival whirling on its heated wheels.
They clambered up and left the vale behind.
It drizzled, and the sharp frost glazed the rocks,
And Phoebe would have fallen many times,
But for the helping arm of nimble Tom.

They reached the ridge, the juncture of two roads ;
A barrier athwart the ridge's vent
Was placed to fend off straying sheep and kine,
And at the barrier they paused for breath.

Tom, with a jest thrown in, said, "Be my wife !"
"Your wife !" said she, "you'd melt the chairs in
    drink,
"And when the liquor's in, the fist is hard ;
"No, no, I will not say, I love you, Tom."
At the last words, a man come leaping down,
And, breathless, at the turnstile, Robert stood
And panted, "Phoebe, take the upper road ;"
But sprightly Tom laughed out, "Grown cautious, Bob?"
"Phoebe," said Robert , "take the upper road ;"
That way she went, but paused, and knit her brow ;
"For Tom's sake, Phoebe, keep the upper road."
Then Phoebe through the lower turnstile pushed,
And took her way along the narrow track.
Tom walked beside her : Robert trudged behind ;
The silent mountain frowned above their heads.
Below, sharp rocks gleamed dully in the sun ;
Tom tried to talk, but Phoebe answered not,
And sad and silent, Robert, watchful, trudged.

They reached an angle where the pathway curves,
When, from beneath him, slid Tom's nimble feet.
He clutched at Phoebe, Robert grasped them both.

Too late ! the three shot o'er the frosted cliff,
And lodged against an aged, jutting pine,
Which creaked and groaned beneath their triple weight.
Dazed, stunned, a space, but with returning life,
Two looked to Robert, Robert looked to God,
And flung a swift, despairing gaze around,
Then eyed the cliff and slowly shook his head.
The pine tree creaked and sent down earth and stones
While misty arms seemed rising from below
To pluck their creepy bodies down to death.

" Phoebe," said Robert softly, " take good heart ;
" Let Tom and you shout all you can in turn ! "
Then he went on like one who thinks aloud,
" The tree's roots give, it will not hold us all ;
" Mayhap if two boys come, you'll call one Bob
" And "—his dumb spirit sought relief in words,
And found it not, and so he turned to thought,
And the great depth flung up more cruel arms ;
Men's past mis-judgment camped against his soul,
And then, oh, doubtless, then, God oped his eyes,
And looking far beyond his silent doom,
He saw God's angels on the mountain-side,
And greeting resolution, Peace flowed in.

Then, " Jesu, Lover of my Soul," he sang,
So loud, so clear, a shepherd on the hills
Heard the familiar tune, and ran that way :

But Tom and Phoebe nothing seemed to hear,
Or heard as if some well-known strain should mix
With some deep dream, well-known and yet not real.
Then Robert sang no more, but turned his eyes
Upon the sun, and stretched his mighty arms,
As if to feel their knotty, fearless strength :
Tied Phoebe to the tree, kissed her, kissed Tom,
And springing backward, launched himself in air
And went from mis-conception straight to God.
If the bruised, shattered atoms voiced a sound,
Only the echo, and the hill-fox heard :
Silent he lived, and silently he died.

Who minds the rest? How the old fir-tree held
Till rescue came, and Tom and Phoebe lived
To walk the earth, and weary 'neath the sun.
Tom died a soldier fighting in Natal,
But Phoebe had no son to christen Bob.

A VESTAL

TO-NIGHT let me picture a maiden
    With lustreless, daffodil hair,
And eyes like dull sapphires unladen
    Of tenderness, frigidly fair,
Her neck and her forehead show whitely—
    The cloister has sharpened her chin
Her voice is some metal struck lightly,
    And her winter of soul has no sin ;
A bloom of the hothouse, its whitest
    Too frail for the rapture of day,
And her face looks not brightly though brightest
    When she comes near the altar to pray.
A vision pre-Christian, arises,
    And sharp are the white and blue lines,
Dark faces look out from strange guises,
    The Cæsar 'neath velvet reclines,
Plebeians, Patricians and Matrons,
    Stout Knights, and Centurions gloat,
While two dye the sand for their patrons.
    One's down—and a sword at his throat—
Dread stillness the horror entrances,
    All pause for the signal of death,
While a Vestal, with dead, pallid glances
    Looks down and indraws her calm breath :

Death broods o 'er the ebony ocean,
    Men gazing and fearing, but dumb ;
Till the Vestal, sans warmth or emotion,
    Points down to the earth with her thumb.
All are gone (and the carcass is somewhere),
    The Cæsar to revel and shame,
While the Virgin, slow pallid and dumb fair,
    Preserves the perpetual flame.

DILUCULUM

YOU in the lithing harmony of youth,
Tracking the spring of now sufficing truth,
You, the home-centre storing joys, who dwell
Spite arid days a wholesome limpid well,
Follow me not : These regions poison yield
From which a poison mask shall hardly shield,
Not even yet the time for you to stand
Within the borders of the twi-dawn land
Where all must come, both holy and forlorn.
The land I track is where no joy is born ;
The home of sounds, which wail of nullity ;
A Freedom where 'tis barren to be free ;
The land of doubt, of guess and evil dream ;
Of desolation's melancholy stream ;
Yet in this stream with bitterness imbued,
Let strong men plunge ; ' tis reverence renewed.

Wearing my soul with flesh not yet dissolved
I enter trance, and find myself involved
In spiritual gloom. Where vapors roll
Is sure the test and triumph of the soul.

Then visions come like dew-drops unaware,
They were not ; in a moment, they are there.
A ship, a river moving noiselessly
Confusion, fog, all these appear to me.

I do not see them, yet they happen clear ;
I know them, yet their sounds I do not hear ;
As an intelligence I understand.
Oft in the ship, and oftener on the land ;
A crowded vessel pressing under sails
'Tween banks so distant each to each looks pale ;
In the blotched sky above is no pure hue,
No reverential white, no restful blue,
Nor that pearl gray when frost thro' amber hints,
No warming red ; but curdled dubious tints,
Colors uncertain in the bruised mass float,
Uncertain as the ever-tacking boat.

Tacking, tacking, edging, here and there,
Scraping the rocks, touching the shallows bare
With swollen canvass, now with flapping sail,
Tacking, tacking, never to prevail ;
Teased by the wind, by counter-currents rocked,
Tacking, tacking, tacking, always mocked.
Now rounding 'neath a mountain's heavy shade,
Now with the bowsprit brushing through a glade.
Now scarcely moving, now with cording strained,
Tacking, tacking, scarce an inch is gained.
And shall we ever face the glowing west,
Diluculum ! the ancient way is best.
Into the dark from shade to thickening shade,
Here, too, have come the "Matron and the Maid,"
Elastic childhood and deliberate age :
Bold Saul, the chief, mild Samuel, the sage ;

Moving through darkness, knowing as I'm led,
The naked wakefulness of being dead.
My senses fade, on spirit cease their hold,
Their powers shrivel, and the soul grows bold.
This is death road, this is the common goal.
God, from the tacking vessel lift my soul.

BEFORE DAWN

THE stark dead hour which comes twixt night
          and morn
      Ere flow and yet past ebb. Exhaustion numbs
The stagnant springs of Nature : all forlorn
      The last grains of existence fall ; or comes
Creation ever near to turn the glass
      And watch the quickened flow. Now passions dead ;
Now deep in mines falls rock in loosened mass ;
      Now watchers reel : o'erwhelmed in heart and head
Long for the morning. Life and spirit wane
      And even love has ceased, dread fills the room ;
Hiss, creak, and dropping start the weary brain
      Unvital air is pregnant with the tomb.
Life's pendulum beats slow, pain reaps its crop
      Strong pulses slacken, and weak pulses stop.

DAWN

EXPECTANT night is heavy with the day,
  Through dumb streets, where a shadow
   makes a stir,
'Neath silent stars, I take my solemn way,
  And echo tracks me like a slinking cur.
Beyond the duskèd pier, in moons waned light
  Soft sleeps the silvern dull but mighty stream.
Against the Northern Sky, in massed up might
  Fleets loom gigantic, hull and mast. We steam
And shatter with our prow the sheet of glass,
  Distort the mirrored city, with its spires—
A huge black steamship, as we lonely pass
  At morn bound sea-ward, opens up her fires:—
On the white calmness ruddy glare with shock
  Bursts like a lion leaping on a flock.

THE CUP CELLINI CARVED

A MERRY call arrayed them on the plain ;
    Dance cheerily, trip lightly, nymphs, O
    sing
And chant to Pan ; and swing the rose-twined chain
    Of grace and perfume.   Dance ! let rapture string
Your drowsy limbs, now lulled by odor's rain,
    As moth in Daphne's depth forgets its wing.

Dance ! 'tis the hour ; on slow and scented wing
    Floats careless zephyr, coaxing dell and plain
And eglantine to ecstacy ; the rain
    Has passed with benediction ; thrushes sing ;
From far leap swains, to join the swaying string,
    While lusty life throbs through the pulsing chain.

Dance ! as ye dance, bind on the wine-wet chain
    Of faint fresh roses.   Dryad spreads soft wing.
Throw back a chastened sound of song and string ;
    For now the smell of honey floats the plain.
Swell ye the anthems, for the while ye sing
    From sacred udder flows the tepid rain.

Dance ! heads are raised as tulips when the rain
    Has passed, the revellers twine in rhythmic chain
Till Pan's pipe trills (while priests exulting sing),
    Sharp, strident shrill, on languid thralling wing,
The note which cheers the gods usurp the plain,
    And rousing nature, stirs life's hidden string.

Dance ! through the years surround me with your
    string
    Of happiness, oh ! let me feel the rain
Of Attic influence, while o'er the plain
    I toss with you the ever-scented chain,
And reach content, upborne on Hebean wing,
    And taste the cup of Pan, and hear him sing.

String, lutes, no more, glad life has left the plain.
    There's treason in the rain, for small drops sing
Treason in singing thrush, its wild wing chain.

A SERMON AT NOTRE-DAME

THE limes of the Tuileries blooming,
    Benisoned air with their sweets :
While the bands played the march from Norma,
    And girls sold Spring in the streets.
In Paris,—the proudly luxurious,—
    Where limpid Seine flows to the sea,
Pleasure and passion were gathered,
    " At rumor of feasting and glee ; "
And art, too, is fêted in spring-time,
    Then luxury makes an advance ;
May comes, and the Epicureans
    Receive all the artists of France.
The Louvre, with its myriad pictures,
    To most of us bade hope depart :
But our giants walked on in the knowledge
    There's always a higher in art.
That evening ease banished arts' furrows,
    And thinking was turned into mirth,
For the wit of the ages was feathered
    By the wittiest tongue of the earth.
Then we wearied of sallies and lightness,
    Of playing with facts like a cat,
And some one set Chartres and the Andes
    Opposed to our shuttle of chat.

Then cried a Parisian, '' Let's see it,
  '' We need an excuse for a walk.''
For Notre Dame's shadow had risen,
  And solemnized riotous talk.
Notre Dame ! So it was in the morning :
  How it grew as we paced the bare floor !
Times unnumbered we'd looked at the wonder
  Though we never had seen it before.
But when we came down from the tower,
  The people had gathered, and straight
A young priest stood up in the pulpit,
  And '' noblesse oblige '' made us wait.
A voice with calm power behind it,
  A man unpretentious but tall,
His text, '' Rich and poor meet together,
  And our God is the Father of all.''

The Sermon

The rich, rich artist and the poor, poor priest ;
The first is rich in art and what art brings :
The last is rich in truth which makes for heaven,
Speed we, my children, down the track of art
And see an image of the heavenly road.
Behold ! this artist with his mobile youth
Responsive to the pictures Nature paints ;
Give him a pencil, all day long he draws ;
Refuse him brushes, and a pointed stone
Becomes his graver, rocks to him are plates.

Not yet beneath the rule of perfectness,
In haste he catches, snatches at all shapes,
His early burgeonings are dewed with hope
That what he mimics, he shall master next.
He calls Art mine, and says of Rubens, "we."
If this were all my children, if he died
Before performance, dissipated dreams,
Paintings were lost, but his young path were joy;
The joy of being Michael Angelo,
Without the anxious care of toil-worn years;
He does not die, he seeks to canvas thought;
Questions arise; the work-a-day begins.

This joy of living is not art's alone;
To eat sweet morsels, and to sleep unvexed,
Belong to every little child of man;
His open mouth is seldom left unfed.
The mail of doubt is not for his fine limbs,
To his pure eyes each elder seems a god.
Oh, careless joy! Wax nature to forget!
Plastic to make the holiest of shapes
Arrest such lives, ye swell the seraph train,
But earth needs pictures, aye! and earth needs saints.

Constant endeavor grips the artist man,
A picket line of problems guards that camp,
Where hope and longing seek to penetrate;
Mixed motives, complex means confront pure thought.

Now colors' use he strives to understand,
The limitation and the good of shade.
He struggles with stained earths and bastard clays,
Finds no means simple, save to cunning hands,
At times o'er effort creeps this dismal rust,
That all he may do has been better done.
Art drives him on : Now, work a miracle,
Make still lines quiver with the joy of life,
Alas ! he's found new toils, but not new strength ;
Now he must know the thought beneath the smile.
" Teach me true art ; " he cries, and finds that truth
Mothered by some great art academy.

The young man wakes to question, doubt and toil.
Naked he stands, bereft of careless joy.
He cannot kill sharp questions if he would ;
And by earth-means these problems must be worked.
'Gainst truth, contends the doubt of what is true ;
Through dull earth-glasses, he must see the sun ;
The Milky Way, a band 'cross childhood's sky,
Resolves itself into a million suns,
Each with its millions of perplexities.
Who shall translate these signs ? The church replies :
" I am thy Mother, I interpret truth."

Now, hard the artist works, but fear has fled ;
Led by authority, he wastes no hours.
Now is he taught how to express his soul.

He knows the good of broken lines and blots ;
He frowns in fresco and refines in oil.
Aided by discipline, by counsel armed,
On, always on, he mounts from height to height.

*   *   *   *   *

From common shapes, and dead antiquity,
The artist presses on to life itself;
And, with divine Da Vinci, hopes to hang
Faces immortal on the walls of time.
If he should flag, two ministers are his ;
Pictures most mighty, canonized by man,
The books of those who spent a life with art.
Assured and led, still on the artist goes,
And wins that immortality called fame.

The seeker, too, has found authority :
A teacher of the soul who greets him fair :
"Surrender nothing, be the things you seek,
I know the roads and means of each fond hope,
Your fit vocation, and its better way ;
I quench false lights by letting in the day ;
Outside weak strokes, I outline what is true,
With me has universal wisdom dwelt,
All higher means and methods, too, are mine.
I am the leader and appointed guide,
The keeper and interpreter of truth.
See, for your solace, on my walls I hang
Pictures of Saints who conquered and achieved,

Giants who fought.   But are your powers few?
My school holds all, has many rooms, and, see!
The Little Master's noblest sketch is here.
If highest wisdom is your aim, then read
These books of mine, by men who lived with God.
Just at this point do art and worship meet,
Here reason and authority concur.
Art goes to nature, comes back to the schools,
And finds they have what nature has and more;
Man goes to reason, labors day by day,
Exhausting body in his weary toil.
Vast calculations! the result is God,
That very God whom all the faithful know.
Who shall lead art?   The great Academy.
Who shall solve doubts?   Our Holy Mother Church.''

*   *   *   *   *

The preacher has gone; noisy tourists
    Have shattered the earnest man's spell.
Then cried out our youngest Parisian,
    '' The Jesuit put the thing well.''

LENT TO THE KING OF THE SEA

A KING on the brink of the ocean,
  Is standing and holding a gem,
A pearl of pellucid whiteness,
  Sheeny grace of his diadem.
He holds it within his fingers,
  Its presence a goodly sight;
While a growing grace he fancies,
  Of a jewel fed on light.

Action and will are with beauty,
  The pearl in his grasp is free,
And slips agleam through the sunlight
  Down to the depths of the sea.
Never a pearl like the lost one
  Shall shimmer in any land;
The diver is plunging downwards
  For a jewel to suit his hand.
'Neath the weedy tangle it slumbers;
  In the ooze of the ocean dark,
It is framed with the golden ingots
  Lost in a pirate's bark.

"Write in our house book," said the king,
  "A pearl of the highest degree,
Of our crown the most excellent glory,
  Is lent to the King of the Sea."—

And in that land for many a day,
When the wise, with a shrug, shook free
From the duties of life, the folk would say,
"Lent to the King of the Sea."

TO MY GODDAUGHTER

Aged Five

KISSING the dainty, dimpled hand,
　　I crush the bow beside her shoulder,
Young Charles—years gone—will seek to stand,
　　Kissing the dainty, dimpled hand ;
His chance must wait, with manner bland,
　　Her friend, though forty summers older,
Kissing the dainty, dimpled hand,
　　I crush the beau beside her shoulder.

ROBERT BROWNING

OFT have I stood where little men complained :
  "Browning usurps the throne of poet-king ;
  Weighting with pedant lore th' aspiring wing."
But King he *is*, the round he wears he gained,
And while an old-time sceptre he disdained,
Yet to his crown some antique glories cling.
The arts are his, so princes ministering
Once served King Edward (at his oar-bench strained)
To be his mate.   Sweep feeling 's keys, at length,
Explore the realms of all philosophy,
Your arc of fancy be as thought's vast swing,
Achieve that love whose essence is its strength ;
Then may you barge our Poet down the Dee,
In fruitful silence hear your master sing.

JUNIUS

"**B**EAUFORT, they called me, born an
          English peer.
          " State tricks, state secrets, often reached
          my ear ;
" I felt the breezes ere they roared as gales ;
" King George leant on my shoulders, babbling tales.
" I had an itch for mystery and fad,
" A joy in mischief, driving statesmen mad.
" I stored ingredients which wound and stir ;
" Planned thunderbolts to vex the powers that were.

" James South was I, a pamphleteer and hack,
" (The canes of knights and lords have warmed my
          back),
" Ready to praise Jove's brow and Hebe's curls,
" To laud a lap-dog, or lampoon an earl.
" My lord's conceits dressed (mixed truth and lie),
" Forging big thunderbolts, not caring why.

" I was Sir Philip Francis, full of guile ;
" I loved a peer, adored a patron's smile.
" A Grub Street hack, spat venom through my pen :
" His periods I rounded now and then.

" I sent the letters, sharp they were, and bold ;
" Defied the Ministers, their spies and gold ;
" Beaufort gave smiles when I my homage paid ;
" I launched the thunderbolts another made.

" Still grouped, we wander in the luke-warm land,
" J. U. N. I. U. S. at your command."

THE COURT AWARDS IT

The Next Day with Shylock

WHY should I stir the dust, or light the logs?
For none will enter, and the fire is here,
Burning forever in my prison-breast.
And none should enter, saving swine and thieves:
My Christian daughter, and her Christian spouse.
Saved! I am saved once more to eat and drink.
I share that tyrany, their tolerance,
Their royal mercy takes my beeves, and throws
The mumbled bone of bent and beggared days.
They strip me bare, oh, tender love! and cast
Over my nakedness, the leper's robe.—
This is not mercy, mercy dwells with worst;—
'Tis gnawing worse, which lets me live to say:
"The curses of my nation guard my head,—
"The spittle on my face now bids me live."
On a proud spirit fell the lash before;
Now, metalled with desert, it cuts the soul.
No tale is told,—no anguish shall be told,
More basely sad, more—God, when hour by hour,
The creature cries: "Oh! just Creator, why?"

Oh, dog! the opportunity was thine
To face the crowd, which, though it hated, feared;
And take the guilty flesh with even hand,
And show their justice what their justice is!

Wail not for that, but rather tell thyself
The cavilling court had birthed one cavil more.
A hundred hands had plucked away thy steel ;
Thou might'st not.   Never Jew found Christian
    just.
Oh, had I dared to dash the court aside,
Under the fifth rib strike, and end it all !
And do as they do,—say the man was cursed,
And then proceed to execute the curse.
I could not strike ; but could I not defy ?
It asked for manhood ; could I be a man,
Hunted from childhood, terrified by wrong?
Go ! Drive the ham-strung war-horse to the charge !
Pluck out men's eyes and say, " Behold the sun !"
Then bid me smite the robber of my thrift,
When he has beaten out my manhood first.
Outrage and wrongs ! Yet Leah used to say :
" Thy desert has a well, it has some shade."
The shade is passed ;—a thief defiles my well.

Yet verily, how little are my wrongs
With what my driven nation has endured !
Because she's proud—is she not patient-proud ?
Fast rain the buffets, deeper bites the lash.
It is my mother, scourged and put to shame,
She owns my tears, she occupies my pain.
I follow in the train,—she drags the car—
The rain is in my face,—she sinks and drowns.

I'm old, forsaken,—happy men grow old,—
And aye, inherit all that troop, age brings :—
Aches, weakness, tears, and manners out of date.
But I had days, some Purim in my youth,
Leah loved me ; I was needed once by Jessica,
Too, Tubal sought me and the Duke lacked coin.

We have one bliss, we die.   The Nation lives,
Though struck and shaken by three mighty waves
Because she kept a Zion in her soul.
Two billows past, and Judah walked dry-shod,
But oh ! the third endures, its darkness grows.
Oh, Venice, cruel City of the Sea !
Oh, treacherous rover, with thy bait of law !
Where shall I seek the harvest of thy deeds ?
In Nineveh, forgotten of the foot ?
In the bare bricks of toppled Babylon ?
Thy trade shall dwindle, and thy pride shall fall,
The strong man's foot shall be upon thy neck.
The Jew shall see it.   Nineveh was great,
Tremendous battlements, tumultuous ships,
A vast of treasure-spilling palaces.
I hug the joy of Nineveh in dust ;
I kiss the sands, which smother out her lines,
Revenge ! it feeds me 'tween the throes of fear.
Shall I not take ?   Shall I not harvest mine ?
Alas ! our sad, sick lives are all the same ;

Bondage, it is the echo of our fate ;
Building, but building nothing for ourselves,
A little heap, the fruit of frugal days ;
A little shelter,—then all gone but hate.

Gaze, men ! we, too, are men—upon the scars
The surface-wounds of tortured Israel.
Rome was the first, she trusted in her spears,
Oh, God, the Lord, thou hast remembered Rome !
Have any suffered ? We have suffered more.
Scattered ! in every nation sold as slaves.
The Gentile babes have had their conscience taught
To link abomination with the Jew.

It might not be ! The Hebrew hunt began ;
The sport of cruelty, the spoil of kings,
Our nation ran the gauntlet of the world,
Down hatred's track we fled with bloody feet !
They even turned our children into spies—
The daughter ! (Jessica has even been).
With Hebrew riches over Hebrew dead,
They purged from Jews the City of the Jew.

O, Lord our God ! because thou art the Lord,
With pestilence and fury slay thine own ;
Deliver, God, those fugitive-parched mouths
My Christian ducats nevermore shall feed :
The worn-out pasture-ground of pious kings,
Those battered foot-balls of a cruel world ;

We are oppressed.   So be it, yet we know
No nation that oppresses Israel,
Inherits peace, and good, and length of days.

O, Judah ! O, my people excellent,
Were there no drops of fatness all thy days ?
Thy first, thy spring, thy origin was proud ;
The chosen people, none can filch that crown,
The salt which kept Creation from decay.
Thy sacred race began when time began ;
Thou art a little people great in soul,
Because the Jew was ever born to hold
The lamp of truth, and light a naughty world,
His will was stubborn, and his limbs were brass.
Wisdom was his, and judgment as a god.
Hate was his portion ; spite, his heritage :
As God is God the just shall shine.

Base fool !

Has Shylock any portion with the just ?
When Israel sitting in the realm of peace
Recalls the vanished night-mare of her wrong,
Of Nineveh, and Babylon and Rome ;
Of Venice, spat at, rotten and despised ;
Then, lowest in the lowest pit of scorn,
Shall Shylock, son of—Shard ! thou hast no sire :
No race, no tongue, no future ; thou art torn
Out of the book of common fellowship ;
Set in a lone of loathing, Shylock has
Nought with the living, nothing with the dead.

A NOCTURNE IN GRAY

A LOWLAND where the mists rolled night and
morn ;
Only at noon the acrid drought dust lay,
Then rising, turned the weeping willows gray.
Lone was the house in whose dull stack was born
The thin white smoke of anthracite.   All lorn
A mocking bird, which echoed nothing gay,
Sang, from an arbor.   There was breath of hay
Which might have voiced Japonica's white scorn,
And dusky grape bloom gave out unctuous scent.
There lilies swung their censers 'neath the skies
While nervous—stepping forward, round, and back
A tall girl clad in clinging dullness, went,
With thin white lips, and chilling handsome eyes ;
Gray eyes, thought-bent upon the moonlit track.

WHAT WILL YOU DO WITH THE CHILD?

A Christmas Thought

ON his staff Caius leaned, and through the gar-
    den went;
    Red roses thronged the ways, all scented, hot
    and bent,
Rich splendor everywhere, sweet nooks for sport and
    mirth;
But Caius wandered on, all sated with the earth.
There came to him a boy, whose ringlets sunbeams
    shed,
Not Ganymede, this youth, for all the gods were dead;
The stripling bore a babe, with face exceeding mild;
No Roman, be ye sure had fathered such a child.
" The Highest sends this Babe, so give to him your best,
" Take solace from his smile; his very touch means rest;
" This is the gift of gifts"—the patient Infant smiled—
" And God will deal with you, as you deal with the
    Child."
And so the infant Christ to pagan Rome was brought.
A holly shaft I speed, and tip it with this thought:
As yearly in our hearts is born the infant mild,
Our God will deal with us, as we deal with the Child.

TO BE PONDERED

REST, color, and substance, the caravans
  deemed
  This old eastern town ; full of hurt ;
Where the dates grew fat ; and the wells were clear ;
  A city of jewels, and dirt.
Though Christian in name it had lost the Lord
  In baits and devices of lust.
Was there righteous man ? Was there yearning for good,
  Save some youth who had hours of disgust ?

There was one, a priest, who met six in the tombs,
  While a singer (as mask), sang of wine,
To hide the weak voice of the priest when he prayed :
  Whose face on this night was ashine.
" My brothers ! " he cried, " In this city accursed,
  Where kindness is only a sneer,
The Glory of God has illumined my soul,
  The day of Jehovah is here."

Was here ! At the blending of morning and night,
  The soul of that prophet had fled :
For the plague rose up with the awful sun,
  At noon the six others were dead.
Men died in the chamber, and died in the street,
  The youthful, the stalwart, the old :
One fled to the desert, one fell on his face,
  One counted his jewels and gold.

One died in his lust, one died at his meat,
    One drank and while drinking was dead :
One twin turned black at his mother's breast,
    The other was starved when she fled :
Till a maniac Moslem set flame to the town.
    Twice twenty were saved, and the rest
Were burnt with their mansions, their gear, and their
       gems,
    Thus vanished the terrible pest.
And they built a mosque, for the Christ was lost,
    I think He had never been found.
Then " Allah " they cry and Mohammed's name
    Is hailed, as they break up the ground.

The truth universal this legend contains,
    With years shall become less vague,
" Let Allah be praised for the sword of the Lord,
    " Jehovah be blessed for the plague."

ANY NEWS FROM GETTYSBURG

THE world was eager for our news,
 And freedom trembled nigh,
A day we rode, a night we rode,
 Again the sun was high.
We galloped past the unstacked wheat ;
 The day was hot and fair,
When "Hark!" my comrade cried, "the guns !
 "They've gripped, and we're not there."
On ! On ! but this is Gettysburg,
 For men swarmed like a sea.
Near gallant Doubleday at last
 Beneath a maple tree.
Behind me wounded men, and some
 Who'd heard their final call.
The turf was ploughed, the trees were topped,
 By shot and minie-ball.
Then, on, my glances roamed afar,
 Past kine and stack of hay,
Past battery which held our front,
 To woods a mile away.
And save sharp-shooters dropping shots,
 Noise from the scene had fled :
The guns were charged, the ranks stood firm ;
 A bird sang overhead.

Two tombing signals from the right,
    A minute, was it more?
Then fiercely from the circling hills
    The Southern guns made roar.
A hundred locomotives shrieked;
    A thousand serpents hissed;
The hellish shells seemed everywhere
    To flutter, moan and twist.
Thud! Thud! on right and left I hear
    The whooping shriek of death:
Fast, faster, falls that devil's hail,
    Quicker than men draw breath.
Two thousand tortive Southern balls
    In fifteen minutes fly;
Two thousand fiends, the Union guns,
    Belch grimly in reply.—
In fifteen minutes, hundreds fall,
    And heroes win their crown:
The battery in front is hushed,
    Horse, men, and gun go down.
Death answers death, as wheeling guns
    Like throttling bloodhounds leap;
The Union guns relax and then
    A moody silence keep.
Skyward a powder wagon flies,
    Is freedom stricken dumb?
And 'mid the hush of Southern guns
    I saw the gray-coats come

Like joyful hunters marching on,
    In ordered close array:
Full fourteen thousand chosen men
    Make rapid, steady way,
Not slow, not very fast, but firm,
    A blazing line of steel
Draws near our front: a splendid sight
    To see each column wheel;
Then, from above, our batteries
    Pour death on Pickett's line,
But on they come, through smoke I see
    Their leader's sword outshine.
Our men a low-aimed volley pour,
    The gray are lying thick,
Yet, with a mighty vengeful bound,
    They charge at double quick:
Covered with blood they near our line,
    On, on, without a pause,
And should they reach that clump of trees
    Down sinks the Union cause.
With muskets clubbed, man fights with man,
    Each private is a Cid:
The North will never give an inch,
    The South will die—and did—
Still fighting in a mix-up mass:
    All struggling but the sped.
A Southern private leaps the wall,
    And by the clump falls dead:

A battery comes madly down,
  From hill to hill is dropped,
The regiments are raging on,
  And Pickett's charge is stopped.

Of those who strove to reach the trees
  Few saw another sun :
And sick, I turned and left the field,
  But Gettysburg was won !

WHY STAND YE GAZING UP INTO HEAVEN?

WHY peer ye up into the blue
    With speechless ecstasy,
While pestilence is on the earth
    And tempest on the sea?
For all must tread the lower peaks
    Ere they deserve the sky;
The choir of heaven may not endure
    The discord of a sigh.
This earth is travail, dreams may be
    The toys of that new birth?
But earth must rise to heaven, no more
    Will heaven return to earth.
On deep and dark foundation stones
    The airy turrets rise;
Love's ladder rests upon the earth,
    Its top is in the skies.
Not in the blue the sense is won
    That ye would seek to win.
To us remains a vision here,
    God's Kingdom is within.
Yet even here in sometime night
    When silence seems profound,
The swift aurora of God's love
    Shall flash from bound to bound.

THE BLISSES OF LIGHT

" A flight of birds struck a signal tower and perished "

BRIGHT atoms of song on the wide pavement
          lay,
       From a red-throated humming-bird, tiny
          and gay,
To a plume-tufted black-bird, with gold on its crest
     Like ointment of Aaron o'erflooding its breast.
O, think of the forest, expecting this troop !
     Can a beech miss a bird ?   Will a branch or two
          droop ?
But see the birds, fervid and fluttering bright,
     And preening their plumes for a thousand-mile flight.
As the Mexican maiden her Angelus sings,
     The upper air stirs with the flapping of wings,
And bits of the rainbow are swimming in space.
     With the hurry of panic begins the long race.
Some chirping, some songless, all questing the light ;
     And there is the redstart, 'tis grace in full flight,
The king-bird whose courage replaces soft tone,
     The titlark, the robin, and songsters unknown,
Flying northward, to whom the black night is no bar,
     Till out of earth's bosom ariseth a star ;
Then blind with its glaring, and dumb with its bliss
     They hurl 'gainst the beacon and die of its kiss ;
Instead of the future environed with fright,
     The flight of desire, the blisses of light.

BESIDE THE ARRAS

A MIGHTY hall which none may see,
 Unsmit by awe and majesty :
 Men pace it with a timid dread,
Its vastness checks a monarch's tread ;
Recessed, it keeps the sun aloof,
Light fingers at the vaulted roof,
And every faded fresco hints.
See how the fateful arras glints !
Three score and ten our mortal race,
A thousand years have touched its face ;
Could all which dusked that cloud reshade,
How rich a Froissart ! louting serfs dismayed ;
Infants that leaped : proud heralds, bearing peace,
Robed Nuncios, Knights of the Golden Fleece,
The stately moving minuet ;
Crossed, pulsing, shadows of some sword-matched fray,
Bowed heads, the coffin on its dullish way—
Wild tossing hands, a fierce unmannered press,
And the mob drunk with that strong wine, success,
Yet for a moment huddled, spell-bound, tense,
At the great pomp of haught magnificence.
Yet that vast hall itself is dwarfed
By mountain's majesty,
Like death beneath the spaceless feet
Of dim eternity ;

For the hall sleeps
'Neath the unchanged upleap of awful mount,
Which chills the valley with its shade,
And awes the stranger,
With o'erhanging rock-tons held by miracle,
Checked ere they plunge
Over the edge of purple mountain heights ;
Vast heights which seem to breathe with whisper of
    pine wood,
Mote of an hour, be good, be good !
To prayer ! to prayer ! atom obey !
Why ache and plot ?   Life is a day.
O dread proud arras, thou too, hast a song,
Choked with the dying feudal dust of wrong.

Store worm ! Spin wheel !
Embroider, eye and hand !
In sunlight come and go, O shadows grand,
O man, O shadow, watch your fellow shades !
They move ! they flit, are passed !
Where bideth strength?
Time rags ; moth frets the curtain's self at length.

The fears of false convention pass,
I do not dread thee, bold, blind mass !
Speak soul ! thou livest not by bread ;
And thou hast words which must be said.

Rich tint, proud stone and height atoned
Not soul, t'was dizzy head which groaned.
'Twas mine bestowed, 'tis I bestow
Thy force to frown, thy power to glow.
Thou art an ancient, awful whole,
And yet one seedling of man's soul.
I think that God may take delight
In cataract and staggering height,
But shall He blanch and stand dismayed
Beneath the bubbles His breath made?

THE SIEGE OF CALAIS

FROM noon till night the English shafts
　　Flew till it seemed to snow :
From Crecy down to Abbeville
　　King Edward chased his foe.

Lord Cobham counted France's loss ;
　　Flags eighty, princes ten,
Twelve hundred chiefs who wore the spurs,
　　And thirty thousand men.

They made a truce to hide the dead,
　　And then, with death and flame,
The English host, advancing fast,
　　To Calais' bulwarks came,

And straitly hemmed the city round
　　With trenches, tents, and streets,
And market-place of wooden huts,
　　Where merchants sold their meats.

And when stout Calais' governor
　　Thrust out two thousand souls,
In dread of dearth and pestilence,
　　King Edward sent them doles ;

He gave them conduct through his lines
   With sterlings twain for alms ;
And for such noble charity,
   The grateful folk sang Psalms.

With fray and foray went the siege,
   A toilsome winter long ;
For Marant's ship brought scanty food,
   And Calais' walls were strong.

Then England built a castle great
   Of wood, a mighty mass,
And from the city to the sea
   Nor ship, nor gull, could pass.

And right a-top of famine sore,
   Which pinched both churl and chief,
The townsmen saw King Philip's host
   March off, nor bring relief.

And when the last French banneret
   Was hid by wall of sky,
All Calais' streets were full of woe,
   Of groan and grievous cry.

It moved the governor, DeVinne,
   Who death and dearth had braved ;
He slowly climbed the ramparts high,
   For parley feebly waved.

"Sir Walter Manny," Edward said,
  " Now get thee quick to horse;
" My message carry to the town,
  " And crush it with remorse:

" If they, for all, a pardon seek,
  " I swear by spurs and crown,
" Their six best men must bear to me
  " The keys of fort and town:

" Barefoot, bareheaded they must come
  " Before the sun is high,
" With hempen halters round their necks
  " Like traitors shrived to die.

" If they delay, I'll sack the town,
  " And slaughter young and old."
Then gallant Manny hailed DeVinne,
And Edward's mandate told.

DeVinne then bade some dong the bell;
  And to the market place
Crawled all the trembling crowd to hear
  King Edward's cruel grace.

Straight spake bold Eustace of Saint Pierre
  " To me is Calais' dear,
" It were a shame to let all die
  " By sword or famine here:

" If six men's lives can save the rest,
    " My faith on God I fix;
" He'll keep my soul, and here I name
    " Myself among the six."

Up rose a cry, surprise and joy,
    And many eyes were dim;
They shouted, wept, and kissed his feet,
    They could have worshipped him.

Quick said John Daire, the prosperous,
    " By Eustace I will stand :"
The brothers Wisant cried aloud,
    " We, too, will join the band."

Ere noon they reached where Edward sat,
    And on their knees fell down;
" Have mercy, king ! We merchants yield
    " The keys of fort and town."

Most fiercely Edward eyed the men,
    Of mercy making scoff:
"Summon the dooms-man here," he cried,
    " Their heads be stricken off."

His Queen, who fought the Scots, was there;
    She knelt upon her knees;
" O gentle sire, to see your face,
    " I've dared the cruel seas.

"Ne'er have I asked a single boon !
  "These citizens have wives,
"For my sake and thy quickened son,
  "I ask for these men's lives !

"Ah ! Lady !" Edward said, "Rise up
  "Again a victor stand !
"Do what you please with these six men ;
  "Their lives are in your hand."

Philippa fed and clothed the men,
  And ere the feast was cold,
She sent them back with brightsome hearts
  And benison of gold.

The names of Queen Philippa fair
  And this undaunted band,
Upon the roll which God approves
  Gold-writ shall ever stand.

LEAVES FROM A WOMAN'S LIFE

THE Outrés' yearly meeting—what a list !
Doctor, Free Lover, Free Religionist,
Painter and Actress—most played roles
compact
Of flame or fuss, disowned if word bore act.
(Be it resolved, " Dirt's matter out of place,"
And yet, to almond soap they trust their face.)
Papers were read, " Long hair the badge of slaves."
" How reverence is fit for fools and knaves."
The Countess went too far (" Sin but Disease")
For even Nature has its decencies—
Shadows, concealments, night has always been—
A nasty thing, her hands are never clean.
" Woman " (was mine) " as rated by the Jew"—
I wore my clinging surah, baby blue,
With old point dripping at the throat and wrist ;
My paper wasn't much—why, someone hissed !
The Countess wore her draggled Nile green tulle,
A dowdy thing, the Countess hates all rule,
A Nihilist, defying and defied.
She's cause-vowed though (or was it wounded pride ?)
A cousin of our hostess, Moltyn Vere,
Had called us,—he's a poet living here.
A Club whose chief is Woman-world-can-dare,
Who rights great wrongs by howls, and beating air :

Claiming, like Jack, the right to break his crown
Tumbling, like Jill, the hill of reverence down :
The Countess drew us from our usual ruts,
She flayed the poet : how her fine lash cuts !
" He sits," she hissed, " perverting thought to
    trope,
" At centre of a great kaleidoscope.
" And friend and foe, and had he wife and boy,
" The bits of red and blue that give him joy,
" He knows love as he knows that art and this,
" From kissing, turns to write about a kiss ;
" O ! he's religious (a cat-fearing mouse) :
" His soul is like a Benedictine House,
" Where prayer-bells ring, and waves of incense drift ;
" While in the parlor sit Voltaire and Swift,
" And Balzac cheek and jowl with Rabelais ;
" But this is Moltyn Vere's religious way."

The room was hot, the talk was trite and dead,
The Countess—crimson rage strove with her red—
I mused : now hear my musings, they are wise,
Besides, they prove our sex can moralize ;—
Is this thy end, O Ideality ?
Are these thy regions luminous and free ?
Years gone, I'd whisper with a nod of head,
Some day I'll sup on hot crusts of new bread.
Later, the man I wed, I used to say,
Soul, body, heart, must carry me away.

Last year, at twenty-one, my quest of mind—
. Some day I'll spread my wings I faithed, and find
Myself in body, out of body, caught
Up to the region of pure working thought :
Another dream, when some day should have come
Languor and sex were factors in my sum.
Some day recedes, though never lost to sight,
Our body is a clog, and a delight ;
When rich blood courses, reason's put to rout,
Toward the things of sense we blossom out ;
And I confess my body makes me sing—
A pear-tree must bloom, beautiful in Spring :
A brief, delicious heritage is grace,
I pleasure in the smooth white of my face,
In dancing limbs, in shot gold of my hair.

Out of the hot room I stole down the stairs.
From the broad steps, mixed with my thoughts, spied
    grain,
Smelt fruit, saw devious life : 'twas like a strain
Of Browning, which we thread and glimpses see
Of Nature, life and immortality—
And through the medley, as in Browning's song,
A voice rose up, rich, confident and strong.

" The Countess," said the voice, then with slow breath,
" God's merciful when poisons smell of death.
" Countess ! the very title seems to be
" A sort of watchword to witch deviltry ;

" Her fierce raw speeches have a smell of taint ;
" Her hair is tangled, cheeks are dabbed with
    paint.
" Down to the Congo's wild beasts lurking brink
" Comes timid antelope at times, to drink.
" So there's a girl, how came she in their crew?
" More beautiful than lilies sphered with dew,
" Her shading eyes are manifold in hue,
" A sense of brilliant black o'ershades the blue ;
" Mutinous brows, and lips which plead forgive ;
" A skin with tints of ivory which live
" Perchance, she lacks the motherhood repose,
" With her "—Here to his brow the color rose ;
My color too, I felt my white cheeks flame,
As round a buttress of the hall he came.
Both brain and brawn (like Esau he was tall)
It takes to make a poet after all.
I felt he caught his breath with pleased surprise,
He knew I'd heard, he saw it in my eyes—
He held my eyes, and searched, and took his
    toll,
Who has not felt the force of out-put soul?
Onward he walked, and closed his speech (to me)
" With her—true complement of soul would be."
His look conveyed a presence to my brain—
The Countess called this power in motion plain—
Sneer at St. Peter's, it won't disappear,
The Countess cannot sneer down Moltyn Vere.

I've met him since, again, and yet again ;
He's tireless, strong, pellucid as the main ;
I'm sure he has a soul, I'm sure he's pure,
But of his heart, I wonder, am I sure ?—
The bees, when Winter warms to Spring, will go
Out of the hive, and settle on the snow,
For all white things are flowers to them—they
    die !
He warms the brain, and satisfies the eye—
From the heart's blossom, scent and honey flow,
The soul puts forth the fresh pure strength of snow.

My man !—ennui has fled ; his kiss makes clear—
The Countess, peste ! I'll write her drivel here.
" Cherie ! the large brained are our sex's curse :
" Beware the man who has a mind to nurse,
" A mind which steals the blood from every vein,
" Which robs the feelings to enrich the brain ;
" A mind for which all fancies are reserved,
" For whose leech-sake, the body is preserved.
" Fresh are the herbs, the oil is twice refined,
" With which he soothes and titillates the mind.
" Poetized facts are only forward brought
" To differentiate the meats of thought.
" Such minds have atmospheres, rare, tingling too,
" And crave sensations—Moltyn Vere craves you.
" Of body-nursing-mind, if you be wife,
" Ponder how you must regulate your life ;

" Must hear his yeas, while other his tones drink,
" Keep off the universe to let him think.
" Nor call your own, the marriage ecstacy,
" His poet-soul allows no privacy.
" The crown of love, so daintily empearled,
" You share it with all women of the world.
" I fancy he could die for some great cause,
" Given the daylight and all men's applause;
" His is the mighty joy in things begun,
" The mighty languor when the deed is done—
" My child, you've married a polygamous mind,
" Which makes a confidant of all mankind."

To muse on rapture is to see it wane.
I have it, yet, I ope this book again.

The Countess wound a scroll—Can she be right?—
Around her wedding gift of Malachite.
" Hold him by wit and pique, before him run
" And let him chase a something not quite won."

Again I write : before God's sleepless eye
(My baby sleeps)—Let the indictment lie !
          *   *   *   *   *
A patient in a ward, his hot eyes dim,
Strikes the bruised ankle, or the broken limb
Crying, " You were my joy, and are my ban,
" Be racked for that stout charge at Inkerman."

Rain down past joys, remembrance be 'portuned,
Though like strong scents you irritate the wound :
Though like strong essence you exhaust my air ;
But for my baby drive me to despair—
My little Moltyn, O my boy ! my boy !
Was ever pain the gate to such a joy ?
Birth-given pain, I count it not an ill,
' Tis needful, or the mother joy would kill.
How shall words tell the first month with my boy ?
' Twas deep, divine, unutterable joy.
A baby to its mother ever brings
An offer, and a glimpse of higher things ;
By babe-wings men may rise, but woman should,
The babe avatar is to womanhood.
As weeks slipped by, and when he laughed and smiled
I found my childhood playing with my child.
But there are lilies in my bed of care,
They fade ; not so the plants which drug my air ;
A child might make Inferno's reeking, sweet ;
There shall be no more children at my feet.
And he'll not care (the truth why should I hide ?),
Philoprogenitive-effects once tried.
A clear cold soul ! But tied to such a soul,
Is this the meaning of the Eastern ghoul?
He loved me once, why cannot love endure ?
For months he asked and gave with manner pure,
With dainty seeing naught but what was best,
The psychic deeps relinquished for my breast.

E'en then he had Egerias of mind,
And to their caves oft went, left me behind.
Draping a thought is no crime, after all.
He sometimes asked me how the fringe should fall.
We drifted on until a certain day
I longed for flesh-pots in the usual way.
In Outré hot-bed air I longed to bask,
" A Talk on Women Doctors" was my task,
And then he spake, a kiss had made me glad,
The thing (with icy courtesy) forbade.
O, I obeyed, the pressure turned me stone,—
My name was his, my lips were all my own ;
We lived, he with the pale light on his brow ;
We lived, he ne'er forgot the 'customed bow.

Married a year we were, no girl can live
Indifferent : she'll hate, or she'll forgive ;
He came ; joy in his step, light in his eyes,
And held a paper, sure some love-surprise.
I waited for his " Darling, one year wed,"
And heard (aye, scarce believed, I heard) instead,
And heard, at once my love was turned to hate,
" Triumph ! at last the Temple calls me great."

My boy ! My boy ! You make great sorrow least,
And you are growing, and your will's increased ;
I wish your curls were darker, dear delight,
Your eyes were browner, and your brow less white.

A fire which rages night and day the same,
And I, a wakeful flame amid the flame,
O, for some coolness, pause, O pulsing tide,
That God may hear, and hearing, may decide.
For now remorse and fury round me roll,
I cannot think, and cry with my lost soul,
" Is there no time apportioned to repent?"
" O, blessed Mother, make the flame relent."
The flame with eyes, the flame which dries and sears,
Dries at its source its privilege of tears;
Useless to call upon the rocks and tide,
A sentient soul nor cave, nor ocean hide,
My baby's bed, once refuge from despair,
I dare not seek; for my dead boy is there.

'Tis an old fancy, aye, 'tis truth as well,
Remembered good or bad are heaven, are hell.
Calm comes; I'll plead as I shall plead some day
Before the powers of truth in dread array—
" O God, you solaced me when love passed by,
" Man tried to snatch your gift, judge me Most High."

For two long years, the man whose name I bore
Gave me food, clothing, bows, and nothing more—
He lived in fancies and the shapes of brain;
And I with drugs, free thought and restless pain.
His eyes seemed saying (so I read their speech)
Like one who hails a swimmer from the beach,

" The ropes are up, swim round, and sport, and frisk,
" But not too far, outside is your own risk ;
" I've done my duty, given warning fair"—
Close to the ropes I swam, to make him care
I swam outside ! The Countess gave a course
Of lectures, " Ninety Reasons for Divorce."
I heard him say, " O, yes, divorce of wit
" From decency ; no honesty will sit
" On such a platform."   Then I spoke, ' twas wrong,
" Mon cher ami, of course you've heard the song,
" Not June, but say-so made the mastiff mad."—
He looked at me, but neither fierce nor glad :
" When folks," said I, " for twenty years have ta'en
" A path, a public path it must remain—
" Ages man's thumb has pressed on woman's brain,
" The law of souls forbids it to remain.
" There must be victims ere a cause succeeds,
" No revolution, but some Corday bleeds."
" The revolution fitting type," said he,
" Which, in a wanton, worshipped liberty."
" Wanton " blurred out the image I'd designed,
I dared not answer, for I knew his mind—
Behind the swift vidette of one thought sent,
Marched vast arrays of fact and argument.
" She is my friend," at last I spake with pride,
" She shall not need a woman by her side."
Then he was angry ; " On your venture, mind,
You leave your child's and husband's name behind."

I heard the lecture, spake I scarce knew how ;
Back in the hall I saw his pale cold brow.
How I reached home, and when, I never knew,
But to the library I fiercely flew,
And there, with royal mien and matchless mould
He stood, so still, so courteous, so cold.
O, all of us some time in life are mad :
" The coldly good, " I cried, "surpass the bad ;
" You, intellect ! most women wed a man !"—
Fiercely I spake, and screaming, dropped my fan—
He bowed, and gave it back, and bone from bone
I tore it, turned, and found I was alone.

When languidly I left my room next morn,
I found him gone, the man whom I had sworn
To love, and did not hate ; his thoughtful grace
Dwelt in the brow, played in my baby's face.
From room to room that morn I wandered on ;
He had not left his stick ; gone, all was gone,
Gone as the prints of yesterday on moss ;
What play, what work should fill the pit of loss?

At Outré's meeting none more bold, more free.
I studied drugs, lived in anatomy,
To taste and fashion, scorning to conform
Dismissed were ministers of flesh and form.

Then woe came nigh the only thing I had—
For typhoid rose, and touched my little lad.

And as we lay, he fevered, I in fear,
There came a letter from the Countess, " Dear,
" Your iceberg tyrant—love, it makes me wild—
" Invokes the law to take away your child,
" For this your use of reason he'd refute.
" Conceal the child, 'tis thought he'll gain his suit."
What ! take my boy? my voice rose to a shriek ;
He lay, the fever glowed in eyes and cheek ;
I clasped him, but his hand put me aside,
An action strangely like his father's pride.
Pierced with sharp pangs, I shuddered, held him fast,
And took the potion meant to check the blast
Which drove out life—I understood life's laws ;
I raised the cup, and then I made a pause :
A hellish, lurid, fierce temptation came.
If he who saved his child from woe and shame
By slaying her, achieved immortal meed,
Why should I fear to contemplate my deed ?
The father in him soon would freeze his charms ;
Suppose he died still tender, in my arms ;
He would not grow to hear my name and shrink
If I withheld the draught ; stay, let me think !
Delayed to give it till life almost waned,
My empty arms were filled if he remained.
How long I waited (time has ceased to be).
I heard him sigh, he turned to smile on me
And gasped ; I clutched the draught, sprang to his side,
He smiled again—impossible ! he died.

SAINT IDA'S MOUNT

LOOK at the great bare mountain,
   With snow for a constant crop;
      No girdle of trees,
      'Tis bathed in the breeze.
   Look at the castle a-top,
Bald, if you will; magnificent and grand,
Its sturdy turrets, gales defying, stand.
Bald as a bishop in his robes of state,
Standing in sturdy might both frank and great,
Love-locks he leaves to fops and cavalier;
But his bald brow serene all men revere.

   Look at that leaning window
      Which a zephyr would treat with pish!
      A jest is that front!
      The king once a-hunt
      Promised his fool any wish.
"Stones," cried the fool, "then let the whirlwinds
   squeak
"And cool my porridge; pile them on yon peak."
The king built Falconberg, but if you please,
By royal edict banned forever trees;
That's why disforested the castle rears
Its head now hoary with five hundred years.

Let the gold plate be triple,
   Still verdigris shows some day !
     'Twas gained in a trice,
     It went by the dice,
   And a great fiend came to stay.
A black-mugged Count, who by cogged bones at play
Ousted the fool and stole the place away.
The fool true native was ; we're simple folk,
Fond of the cup, and ready for a joke ;
Tuscan or Greek the Count ; his youth was cold
Baptised in fumes of craft and sweated gold.

Often the ill weed prospers
   Away from its native heath !
     How rabbits will band,
     Destroying the land,
   Save by the fox's sharp teeth
They're thinned ; so villains other villains kill ;
The fierce gray rats, brought from the Northern hill
Will swarm a place and soon out-root the brown ;
So did the cursèd Count possess our town ;
Now in the heights of Falconberg he sat,
Now scoured the streets like any other rat.

They met in the blazing ball-room
   Where all that are noted mix;
     Most fair was the sight
     Of Ida, plump, white,
   The Count was a death's-head on sticks.

Well born and stately, strong as she was sweet ;
She trod our Eagle's Pass with nimble feet,
Her wrist as strong as that wild sailor's—Meier—
Who with one hand slid down our Dom's great
    spire ;
Till once she slipped, was hurt, endured such fright,
That from that time she sickened on a height.

    Once, as he passed, she whispered,
        " Look ! look at the lackey's pride,"
          As a child may cry
          When a snake glides by,
       " When will he capture a bride ? "
Above the music of his train, he'd heard
Her words, and all the venom in him stirred ;
For he had worn the lackey's garb in youth,
And nought hurts more than sharp saw-ends of
    truth.
A lust to kill controlled Count Hugo's face,
And evil found in him a garnished place.

    The quagmire soul that's nesting
      A dozen of serpent's eggs
        Will hatch some, I wis :
        Till force and fraud kiss.
    " Bruise her white arms, crush her legs,
" Drag her from height to height when she is lame,
" Strip her of sympathy, filch wealth and fame,

" Destroy that smile, and turn it to a sigh,
" The sadder that no friend shall then be nigh ; "
But Satan's self suggested, " Make no stir,
" Thou dullard, have and kill her—marry her."

    Mark how the trap he baited,
        He sadness with pique combined ;
           Her wishes to please
           Are half a disease,
        They overcome woman's mind.
He puzzled her, then wooed with all his might,
He wore her chains like one who hugged them tight,
Then as the blind command he calmly said,
" You've ta'en my eyes, by you I must be led."
Grand was the wedding, but the girl was trapped,
The moon soon passed, and Hugo's steel spring snapped.

    All leaden-pale, one morning,
        Along padded corridors,
           Where curtains were placed
           Till sound was effaced,
        Over echoless carpeted floors
He led her to revenge, a low-pitched room,
With marble port carved like a vaulted tomb.
" Now, can your dainty ears," he softly said,
" Detect in anywise your lackey's tread ?
" Here make your nest, enjoy the restful view,
" It is your lackey's wish, Madame, adieu ! "

Yet, as he shut behind him
>The leather-hinged door, close pressed,
>>He sobbed like a child,
>>With gesturings wild ;
>Hatred and love in one breast.
He'd gained the bride by fawnings, tricks and lies,
But her soul's goodness hurt his carnal eyes :
What if he'd gained her, clasped her, bone of bone,
He felt her spirit mixed not with his own.
Smirch her he would, and then, perchance relent?
So curses joined strange weeping as he went.

"Adolfo," her voice was tender,
>It was all caressing and sweet,
>>The curtains thick spread
>>Increased her sick dread,
>And at each tread of her feet
The carpets pulsed, like tiger paw concealed.
She asked herself,— " Will God now be revealed?"
Then stricken as a mourner near a tomb,
She moaned, " Hail Mary ! Oh ! this cushioned room,
" Its cruel velvet stillness makes me wild,
" It is as dire as darkness to a child."

Three of its sides were padded
>With yellowish thick-wrought pile ;
>>The front was all glass
>>And sloped o'er the pass
>(Window to valley a mile.)

Leaning as if designed to let you go
With slip and plunge to nauseate depths below:
A hellish freak had schemed this plague-dyed place,
Whence as you looked you seemed arush through
     space,
And such a stealthy silence palled the room!
All earth was dead, she stayed the day of doom.

Ever at morn and evening
     The Count, to this den of fate,
          Brought delicate cates
          On magnificent plates,
With a voice all soft in its hate,
Entreating her to whisper some command:
And oft with rat-like stare she'd see him stand
Poised on the window-ledge which like a slide
Sloped o'er that cruel death.   So Summer died,
And Autumn drivelled out mid gloom and wet:
And winter came nor was it God's time yet.

God at our need's end meets us:
     One morning there came a frost.
          Ah, was it a dream?
          Or did the Count scream?
     "Devils! ye Saints! I am lost!"
She half awaked, and just above the ledge
Of that swayed window, saw one at its edge

Who (chin and fingers stiff), the coping grasped
But hung in space as he for mercy gasped.
One pause : and she her two arms strong and white
Flung round his tensioned neck and held him tight.

Now, with the chance of living,
He yelled on the brink of doom,
"Help ! Hermann ! Baptiste !
"God ! Devil ! or Priest !"
Never a sound passed the room.
She could not drag him from that shapeless wreck,
So stretching on the floor she bowed her neck,
He clutched her round as drunkards clutch the cup,
With sudden strength she swayed and drew him up,
And at her feet with broken spine he lay,
Nor ever moved but died with sinking day.

Heaven rest his soul ! he died at Ida's feet,
And chancely made confession's foul flood sweet.
The ruined Castle lives the sport of gales,
Goodness has christened well this Queen of Vales ;
Redeemed from mem'ries of the hellish Count,
That's why they call this peak "Saint Ida's Mount."

ACROSS THE BARRIERS

(*Singing Heard*)

Sir Roland

" Doxes, doxes,

" Glorious oxes,

" Spermaceti pie."

So the voice spake when young, so speaks now old :

Some secret vast this childhood's tag must hold.

(*Visitors Enter*)

The Doctor

" Sir Roland Darcy, visitors are here,

" To pay you their respects, (don't be severe)."

Sir Roland

" Ah, gentlemen, your names? You're Mister Spy ?

" Haven't the honor ; gentlemen, don't pry.

" A dotard has some social rights : my fall !—

" Pardon is granted : Pray, be seated all.

" See, on the wall, my chart of moon and stars ;

" That's my world chart, all mapped behind these bars.

" Intellect scale ! A scale for all alive :

" Idiots, five ; a genius, twenty-five ;

" Fifteen, you, sir, a man with prying pate ;

" Fanatic, thirty : I am twenty-eight :

" I've traced out thought and found its end (you nod !) ;
" I think you heard my song ? O, I am odd !
" Not queer, but in the vanguard of to-day,
" Original, unique, bizarre, outré :
" Be honest, says one age ; be brave, another ;
" A third, for liberty will hang his mother ;
" The passion of a fourth, to worship God,
" The fashion of to-day, be odd, be odd.
" What is the first thing ? be original,
" What is the next thing ? be original,
" What is the best thing ? be original,
" What is the worst thing ? be conventional.

" Now, it must be admitted, if you please,
" At birth no human creature has disease :
" If from your birth a voice speaks words to you,
" That voice is real, actual and true.
" Ghosts ! Saul saw Samuel ; you'll not deny
" Blake saw and painted spirit bodies ; I
" Have seen my shade with, (pshaw ! I make no boasts) :
" Ocean has many fish, air many ghosts :
" Delirium's not phantasy untrue :
" Tis seeing more than healthy sight can view.
" The truly present, air-infesting ghost
" To fever-sharpened sight appears the most ;
" Allow a spirit form, you have no choice ;
" You must allow a living spirit voice
" May come to one made keen by fever's blaze ;
" I've had a little fever all my days :

"Not for this gift exceptional, conspired
"The world to shut me up, and Galens hired
"To call me wild ; but, see, I followed truth
"To its end logical, and felt no ruth ;
"Wordsworth and aye the public voice will wage
"That childhood's nearer purity than age.
"But even age (here Hamlet quite agrees),
"Is nearer heaven when on her bended knees,
"And here's the point, — O, Doctor, must you go ?
"I'm sorry : for the point's exactly so.
"You'll come again? Oh, thank you all : I'm glad :
"My Doctor, — (mum, you know !) is rather mad."

(*Keeper to the Visitors, outside*)

"You're welcome, gentlemen, Sir Roland fails :
"Shot his wife dead before the altar-rails.

VEER-WILL-BANE

O F " Veer-Will-Bane " which paralyzes will,
There's less than of the metal yttrium,
In all the wide, wide world, there's not a pound;
" Worara's " opposite, this poison seems :
Worara makes the muscles impotent,
Leaves vision and intelligence intact ;
But Veer-Will-Bane, while stupefying will,
Quickens the muscles, flogs the energy ;
Yet wields the body as a soulless slave
To every uncontrolled and vagrant thought.
Is it insanity? if will is quelled
And all its force centripetal removed,
So that the moral qualities are left
In one wild rout of chaos, and of might,
Till the police, called will, revives to act
With force, and holds the whirling mob in hand,
And brings the system back to ordered rule?
Am I rhetorical? Then blame the drug ;
I've tried the Veer-Will-Bane upon myself,
And closely noted how the poison works.
Two doctors' observations piece my tale.

On Tuesday morning, in my cabinet,
We met.   At ten, I swallowed sixty grains :
It had the scented taste of pure Moselle,
And drove the hot blood rushing to the brain,
And for a day I wandered up and down,
Constrained to speak aloud unpleasant truths,

And thoughts sarcastic, such as cut and tear,
I told the doctors what I thought of them :
How Doctor Dubitanti loved his fees,
How Saranack in practice overdrugged,
With fifty other things, which if believed,
No sane man ever dreamed to put in words.
Ere day was done, I reached the second stage,
When wildest theories displaced hard facts,
In a Coleridgean vein for hours I spoke,
And used my thronging words to demonstrate
That from the tangled forest-growth of mind,
Replete with virginal luxuriance,
Came forth the Goths of all discoveries
Which, though they crush and trample, ne'er destroy,
But prove the pioneers of better things.
Then, with a rush, I joined that thought with this,
That nervous energy is simple kin
To some electrical phenomena.

Some things I wrote, which pray you briefly scan,
Though they be wild, decide, are they insane ?
I deem they show mind exaltation, with
The loosened pressure of judicial will.

Notes on Divinity

This world of man is like a healthy brain,
Packed with a million multivarious thoughts,
The caravansary of good and bad—
Here come the sage, the savage and the seer,

Imps of the slime, and seraphs of the light,
They come, they go, but, whether good or bad,
Obedient to the keeper of the house,
Obedient to the law of charity,
And so the brain-world goes upon its way,
The bad restrained or fuel-used for good,
Some thoughts are quelled, some welcomed, some rebuked,
And all obey, pay toll to charity ;
And over all, through all, His will is done.

The hours passed on, and then the third change came,
And, baby-like, with trifles, I began
To dally, wafted round with vainest thoughts
Which led me from the house, across the street
Where stood a hogshead by a grocer's door.
At once I called to mind Diogenes,
And, instant, tried to climb within the cask.
By force they led me back again to home,
And as the noxious mists cleared from my brain,
I asked, in shaken tones, "What is to-day?"
They told me Tuesday morn ; I almost laughed ;
"But what is now the hour?" 'Twas half-past ten !
Just thirty minutes had seemed hours and days.
I write this slowly for my hands and joints
Are stiff ; besides, my colleagues say I've aged,
And if my mirror plays no optic trick
My hair since yesterday has whiter grown.
I cannot write more now—my paper swims
Before my eyes, and concentration seems impossible.

A THOUSAND YEARS OF FAITH

ON a big hill, burnt brown and bare
        The massive church arrests the air ;
        Nothing of grace the sunlight lends,
Its heavy lines, the pile offends
With glaring white both eye and brain,
Its hugeness bullies all the plain.
Against the sky it lolls supine,
A rock chipped out by Frankenstein,
Why should men 'neath oppression sit ?
The Colonists are proud of it.
On brain, on tongue its bigness swells ;
Their town's the belfry for its bells.
I creep into its heavy dark
With more blunt masses than Saint Mark
Has pillars— color blotches steal—
I sicken 'neath the lowering ceil.
Not vain the flood, not vain the dark
Which drives the dove back to the ark.
Ere heaviness had struck its blows,
From memory a contrast rose ;
Rheims, too, is vast, but Rheims is fair,
Her groined stone masses float in air !
Spirit in stone ! O, rose of grace,
Epochs have bowed before thy face,
Vast masonry beatified,

Where rapture and surprise abide
Forever dwell unstale, unspent,
Spite long continued wonderment.
Within ! Be still, O, pulse of time !
Within ! How nakedly sublime !
Here solemn music penetrates
The mellow dyes which heaven translates,
Within are aisles of sculptured peace
Where colors raining, never cease ;
Yet spite the windows, one cascade
Of jewels bathing shapes arrayed
In robes whose satined splendors kiss.
Spite, saints and signs and hues of bliss,
Awe struggles with that rainbow flush,
Dread grows beneath that awful hush.
The world is kneeling here unshod,
This is the awfulness of God
Which smites down sight.   Lord lift our eyes
Up to thy loving sacrifice.

    *   *   *   *   *

Then breaks the bubble fancy blown,
Once more I'm tombed in vaults of stone,
But why this clumsy darkness ?   Why ?
A tablet near me makes reply :
I read his name who piled this mass
And understand in part—Alas !
Have men, with each a centred plan,
Dispowered the work of centuried man ?

And will each vie in his short years
With æons, crafts, and hemispheres?
Aye ! As the ages onward roll
This thrusting forth of naked soul
Has plucked at grace with hands astir ;
Who vaulted, tell me, Winchester?
From whose mind came severe Cologne?
A thousand years of faith alone.

AN HEIR OF KINGDOMS ON THIS EARTH
NOT CROWNED

(In memory of our friend J. S.)

WHEN the white light of Jehovah purges
evermore
Darkness and dignities; when matter
wanes,
Like floating vapor at the furnace door,
And only love remains,
Love in whose volumes human sparkles burn,
Those pure desires whose signet is a sigh,
Longings which never found achievement's end ;
Yea something of this song shall be eterne ;
For love indeed has quickened its poor cry,
My friend ! Alas ! My friend !

Fill me to ecstasy with lofty phrase,
O, thou illumined and perpetual might !
Be mine the note of high and holy praise ;
Yet not for him I light
The torch.   He stands 'mid the triumphant train,
A shining spirit and a peer all strong,
A soul transcending where all souls transcend ;
I pour his praises to assuage my pain,
Mine is the sorrow, mine the solace song,
My friend ! Alas ! My friend.

With what compare thee?   On the wings of song
    If I might steal a shadow of thy grace,
I would compare thee with the joys that throng
    Thy now enraptured place.
But like a bird I strike the walls of time,
    Interrogating wood, and earth and sea,
Have ye no royal children? can ye send
    No serried chieftain, lords of the sublime
To swell the pageant of his threnody?
    My friend! Alas! My friend!

All Eden's garden dyes with doubts are sighing,
    And wildly whispers every naked tree,
None, cries the wood to my demand replying,
    More beautiful than he.
Smooth is the birch and big the chestnut bole
    With crimson gloss ashine my poppy glows,
But palms decay and perfumes have an end ;
    My ranks have no example for his soul,
Grand as the beech and royal as the rose.
    My friend! Alas! My friend!

"None," answers earth, from out her shimm'ring
    palace,
    While colors flashed and iridescence stirred ;
I have befitting gems for crown and chalice,
    None rarer than his word.

I have red rubies prince of jewel kind,
    And adamant which flashes back the glow
Of morn, but not in gem nor jewel blend
    Such playful flames as kindled in his mind
Purely surpassing all my flush and flow.
    My friend ! Alas ! My friend !

Thunders from all her pearly caves the ocean
    And smites the clouds with brine ;
My court and bounds have beauty, mirth and motion,
    I claim him wholly mine,
For save my realm the world has nothing vaster.
    My power has no man tamed? and no man can,
And all the phrases by the singers penned,
    The fresh, the free, the strong and mighty master,
Proclaim me Ocean and proclaim him Man.
    My friend ! Alas ! My friend !

But he is crowned, in that let me rejoice,
    In that I conquer space and pass the bar.
He tastes the amaranth, he hears the voice,
    He comes where poets are.
Brave Browning leads his spirit to the light,
    A sudden smile of recognition breaks,
Avon and Chaucer from their dais bend,
    " Welcome," they cry, "you loved and did us
        right ;"
" Welcome," they thunder, till Olympus shakes,
    Thy soul was love, O friend.

All that I am is thine ; what I may be
    Is thine, inherited from days of yore,
For I have shared thy rich humanity,
    O, Master, gone before.
Farewell to fellowship and eloquence
    Farewell, my higher self, my source, my spring,
All these expired with thy passing bell ;
    A little longer be the things of sense,
A little while I struggle, toil, and sing,
    And then no more farewell.